The Imposter Prince

By

Wendy Rathbone

I0608403

**The Imposter Prince Copyright © 2018
by Wendy Rathbone and Eye Scry Publications**

Cover design: Jay Aheer

**A publication by:
Eye Scry Publications**
http://www.eyescrypublications.com

ISBN # 978-1-942415-21-3
TITLE: The Imposter Prince
Author: Wendy Rathbone

© All rights reserved. This book may not be reproduced
wholly or in part without prior written permission from the
publisher and author, except by a reviewer who may quote
brief passages. Neither may any section of this book be
reproduced, stored in a retrieval system, or transmitted in
any form or by any means, electronic, mechanical,
photocopying, recording or other, without prior written
permission from the author, except as exempted by
legitimate purchase through the author's website,
Amazon.com or other authorized retailer.

Address all inquiries to the author at:
wrathbone@juno.com

Acknowledgments

I'd like to give a special thank you to **Jay Aheer** for this book's beautiful cover.

Also, thank you to **Christina E. Pilz** for a wonderful beta-read of this novel.

And last but not least, thank you **Della Van Hise** for help with formatting and uploading all my published books. I couldn't do this without you.

Chapter One

Dare leaned against the padded window-seat, staring out at the world beyond.

The view from the prince's quarters offered a spectacular vista of the Twelve Waterfalls of Brookfall pounding their starry froth into the narrow purple valley below. The falls were a mile away, but he heard through the open casement their wild and pounding roar. He smelled the greenness of the wind they made, and a hint of fresh vastness, like cool rain in autumn just before sunrise.

Castle Brookfall had been built longer ago than anyone could remember. No scroll or book existed to tell of its origin. It stood on a cliff of brown rock, a great, moss-covered palace ruling the misty air with twenty spires, ten towers, and a bridge that branched a chasm to a vast open land of fields and farms as far as the eye could see.

Dare was lucky to live here. He kept telling himself that each day he woke to the beauty around him. Every day he opened his eyes to see the prince's quarters with its lavish, tapestried walls, its silk-woven rugs, hand-carved oak tables and chairs, and the many-colored glass lanterns shaped like moons that hung from the high ceiling. He wore robes of precious silk, even to bed, and had many jeweled bracelets and rings, though he really could not call any of it his own.

A voice came from his left. "Did you hear me? Footstool. I said I need you over here. Now."

Dare turned from the window, eyes half-closed, staring at the blue and gold sun-patterned rug on the floor. When he looked up, all he saw for a moment was a blur of white as his eyes adjusted to the dimness of the room lit only by one oil lamp at the desk, and two candles on a nightstand. One by one the furnishings came into focus, the table, the desk, three chairs, and the bed.

The room contained three doors. One led to a shadowy hall lit day and night by orange-hued oil lamps. Another shut off the small chamber pot room. The third led to a vast closet filled with satin jackets, brocaded vests, dozens of white shirts and black trousers, white and silver cloaks for summer, and heavier ones in brown and blue and red for winter.

Dare's clothing took up only one small corner of that closet. He had three complete outfits for all-weather, some extra shirts with puffed white sleeves, and one cloak, black. One wooden trunk held all his private things including a few books, a stuffed rag-bear from his pre-teen years, ribbons to tie back his hair, a brush, a hand mirror, a small wooden sword, some smooth stones found at a nearby riverbed, and some old glass and metal necklaces that had once belonged to his mother. Nothing of worth, really. The thin silver bracelet cuff his mother had always worn when she was alive stayed on Dare's wrist at all times.

"I said get over here now," said the other occupant of the room.

Prince Darius, who had the same name as Dare but never allowed himself to be called any nicknames, lolled at his desk looking annoyed and bored. He'd been working on a homework assignment from their history teacher. Darius hated history. To be fair, he hated all subjects of study. Dare was the one who usually finished his homework assignments for him, as well as his own, for they were tutored together, as they had been since the age of five.

"Are you deaf, Footstool?"

The prince had his own nickname for Dare. It had started around puberty when Darius, who had always been a surly, bossy playmate, figured out that Dare was merely a servant, there not only to keep him company, and be his companion, but by royal decree had to do everything Darius said. When he figured that out, his bossy nature turned darker and bullying at times. They no longer played the games of children. Now things had taken a dimmer turn.

Prince Darius had been an unhappy child, to be sure, but as a teen he was downright miserable, keeping himself shut away most of the time, hating everything from his father the king to the idea that he might some day have to do real work like running an entire kingdom. He loved ordering servants about, but he did not seem to enjoy life at all. He resented everything.

Now at eighteen, both Dariuses still lived in the same room. Dare had his padded mat at the foot of the royal bed, and a small desk for homework in the darkest corner of the room. As tots, they had looked almost like twins. Now, though they still resembled each other greatly, Dare was slightly taller, much to Darius's displeasure, and his hair was shinier. Where Darius's features were hard, Dare's were pretty. Dare had a sensitive heart while Darius seemed to have no heart, mostly unconcerned about the welfare of others unless he was to gain from the interaction.

Dare moved to the desk until he stood before Darius, inches from his outstretched feet.

Darius looked up at him through thick, black lashes, eyes a lovely dark brown but somehow empty in their gaze. He always looked like he was glaring.

When he didn't immediately speak, Dare said, "Do you need me to finish your homework?"

"No. I just wanted to put my feet up. You can do my homework later." He cocked a half-grin that fell into a smirk.

Dare was familiar with this game of one-upmanship. It was Darius's way of proving who was better, richer. In charge. This act Darius made Dare perform was how he'd gotten this second nickname. *Footstool.*

Dare knelt on this hands and knees and turned so Darius could put his feet up onto his back and rest them there.

"Good, Footstool."

He dug his heels into Dare's back, pinching the scars there. Scars he had from the whippings he received whenever he got fed up and defied the prince. He'd learned quickly to say "yes" to anything the prince asked of him, but once in awhile it was just too hard, and his defiance was punished with a leather whip that made him bleed.

The longest Darius had ever made him play footstool for him was a full day. When he'd finally been allowed to stand, his whole body ached.

Today, he could tell the prince was restless. It wouldn't be long before he'd get up and want to find a servant boy or girl to bully, or demand Dare play any number of games with him that Dare always had to let him win.

Dare tried to stay very still, assuming a mood of unconcern. If he showed any sign that Darius's orders bothered him, it only spurred the prince on to tease, to torment, to torture.

As Dare knelt, Darius began to talk, tossing his head, his voice low and bored. "There's a delegation coming. They'll be here for dinner."

"Oh?"

"Yes. From Shastan."

"Shastan?"

"Yes. Can you believe it? My idiot father thinks he wants to talk peace with them. They're barbarians, you know. I hate them."

"You've never met a Shastan."

"I don't care. They've made war on us in the past. They're completely untrustworthy. Everyone says so. I tried to tell Father but he's letting them through anyway, and breaking bread with them!"

8

"I'm sure it will be fine."

"Good. Then you won't be bothered to take my place at the banquet table, will you, Footstool? They'll probably want to poison all the food!"

Dare lifted his head. He did this all the time, traded places with the prince when the prince felt unsafe. It happened often, for Darius possessed an abnormal paranoia that had gotten worse in their teens, and he despised social events. Dare had gotten good at playing the royal role at public events, and during travels when safety from assassins might be an issue. This wasn't too unusual for the king had a double, too.

"I would be happy to represent you at the banquet."

"You have to be me. And then report back. Tell me everything they say."

"I will."

He gave Dare a tight, hard kick. "You better."

Dare turned his head and gave him a reassuring smile. Darius scowled, then pushed him with his heels.

"You should get dressed, then. Wear my green vest and cloak. And here, take these." He threw three rings at Dare. They glinted in the white light from the window, three mini-stars falling to the floor by his thigh. "And wear the silver leaf crown, too."

"What about your homework?"

He grunted. "Fuck. I'll do it. You better be good, Footstool. You better come back and tell me everything. If you survive the poisoned food, that is."

Dare refrained from rolling his eyes, rose to his feet and headed for the closet.

Chapter Two

The great banquet hall of Castle Brookfall stretched deep and long. Candelabras twinkled all up and down the joined line of tables. Along the walls on both sides of the huge, high-ceilinged room, lanterns of blue, green and gold glass glowed making the entire chamber beautiful and ominous at the same time.

A six-foot dragon sculpture carved from a slab of black marble greeted visitors at the main entrance. Two smaller marble dragons guarded the huge double doors that led to lush and fragrant gardens where guests could wander, or sit on benches and have conversations. More glass lanterns hung from trees, or sat on spikes along the pathways.

Dare stood by the entrance and greeted each new visitor with a polite bow and smile. The king had already been informed that the real Prince Darius had declined to attend. It was such a common occurrence that he did not seem to care.

Dare played his part well. He knew how to behave and speak. He understood politics. He presented a clear and fair-minded image to the group from Shastan.

Late in the evening, after he'd eaten non-poisoned food and laughed with a few of the delegates, one took him aside and said, "Thank you for the fine meal and your welcoming presence. We'd heard rumors that Prince Darius is a terror. But you are a fine and wise young man. May our kingdoms have fair trade and peace at last, for now and well into the future."

Dare replied, "It is all I hope for."

Darius would have never been so agreeable, but Dare didn't care. He was the prince of the moment, and who in their right mind wouldn't want peace?

Slightly drunk on wine, Dare took a walk in the gardens with a handsome male delegate who touched his hair and called him beautiful, though he took things no further. He'd realized at a young age that he liked men in this way, and didn't mind the touches and the compliments.

The evening progressed in a lovely drunken haze of jugglers, musicians and dancers. Until the scuffle.

Dare heard the commotion as he was coming in from the gardens, and arrived in time to see a group of men from Shastan facing off an equal number of the king's guard, swords gleaming in the winking candle-light.

"Enough!" the king said, his low voice echoing off the walls of the now-silent room. "The Shastan delegation will all leave at once, or be thrown in the dungeons to await trial for crimes against this country!"

Dare saw Voy, a servant he had known his whole life, and moved next to him. "What happened?"

"The king was insulted. I did not hear the details."

The Shastan men, including the delegate who'd walked with Dare in the gardens, all left as a group.

Within minutes, Dare could hear, through the front hall, horses in the courtyard and men's shouts. Soon he heard the hooves of horses on cobblestones. The sounds turned to thuds as they passed the high gate and the riders hit the wood planks of the bridge. Finally, the hoof beats receded altogether when they reached the softer grassy meadows. Sentries shouted to one another for a while. A distant horn blew.

The hall was clearing out. The king had already left. Servants moved about, clearing food and plates and goblets away. At the whim of the king, the festivities were quickly over.

Dare had hoped to stay away from Prince Darius's rooms until late, when the prince would be tired and not have the energy to pester him. He moved through the halls and up the winding, stone stairs to the prince's chamber.

But it was still early, and Darius looked up as he entered. He stood by a table near a tray of half-eaten food. He looked bored and miserable. For a moment, but only a moment, his eyes lit up as Dare came into the room and closed the door.

"What are you doing back so early, Footstool?"

"Your father ordered the Shastan delegation away. Someone said he'd been insulted, but I didn't hear any more details."

Darius snorted, then laughed. "I told him they were barbarians. But he doesn't listen to me. I wonder what they said to him."

"I don't know. But he looked angry."

"They probably made some stupid request my father denied, and they got mad over it. Well, maybe there will be war again."

"You can't possibly hope for war."

The edge of a sneer curved at the side of the prince's mouth. "Why not? I'll never see combat. Only ever this boring castle. When I'm king, at least if there's war I'll be able to order men to spy and fight and die for me."

Dare watched him pick up a goblet and drink. Darius set it down licking his lips.

"What?" asked Darius as he met his gaze. "I'd never ask you to go into combat. It'd be stupid to risk such a good footstool, so you needn't worry."

Sometimes, Dare saw hints of affection in the prince. But they were rare, and mostly they happened when the prince wanted something. What would he want tonight?

"So what else happened at the party? Did you eat? Do you feel sick?"

"I'm fine." Dare took a deep breath.

"Well, still there was drama. The Shastans cannot be trusted. Did you meet any of them?"

Dare nodded.

"Come." Darius motioned toward a chair at the table. "Have more wine if you want it."

"I've had enough." Enough to make him somewhat happy during the evening, and a little off-balance. He approached the table, seeing a half-eaten chicken, crisp golden rolls, and a bowl of fresh fruit. The crystal carafe of wine smelled slightly sour. Candles flickered over the scene. He started to sit when Darius smacked him on the arm.

"Not on the chair, Footstool. Kneel."

It was this way most of the time. Why Dare thought it might be different tonight, he didn't know. Always, Darius held out his hand and when Dare reached for it, he got slapped. No matter how hard he tried to be pleasing for Darius, the prince was not the type who made friends.

He knelt and Darius sat.

"First, take off my boots and my cloak. I don't want them messed up."

Dare obeyed, straightening up and removing the cloak, then he carefully folded it and set it in the chair behind him. He sat and removed the soft leather boots, setting them aside.

"There you go," Darius said.

Dare positioned himself so Darius could put his bare feet on his back. He felt the heels dig sharply into his spine and held back a gasp.

"I should have had you take all my clothes off before you completely stunk them up. But oh well. Now, tell me every detail about the banquet."

As Dare spoke, Darius pummeled him with questions. He really did seem to want to know a lot about the evening which was a change since Darius was not interested in much, except complaining.

When he came to the part where the handsome Shastan delegate accompanied him through the gardens, Darius said, "Didn't he do anything more than touch your damn hair?"

"No."

"He didn't kiss you?"

"No."

"You wanted him to, though, didn't you?"

When Dare did not answer, Darius said, "I know you like boys. He could probably sense it. Shastans are rapists, too, you know, and that's what he probably would have done to you if my father didn't have so many guards about."

"But he was nice," Dare said softly.

"It was a trick. Besides, you're mine. You can't trust anyone, you know."

Certainly not you, Dare thought. Only eighteen, and the prince was so jaded and suspicious. Yet it seemed he'd been that way since Dare had met him when they were both children, Darius a child of five going on twenty with empty, empty eyes.

"You have to watch out for yourself," Darius continued. "But you are weak that way. At least you have me to look out for you. I keep you safe, Footstool, don't I?"

Not safe from you. Aloud, he said, "Yes, my lord."

Darius asked more questions. For over an hour Dare knelt on his hands and knees, feeling the weight of the prince's feet. It was as if with every minute they got heavier. The wine had long worn off. The muscles of his back stiffened.

When the prince tired of talking, he said, "All right, get up and go take off my clothes. Make sure you put them out for the maid to launder. I don't want to wear them with your stench on them."

Dare rose to his full height, not even turning to look at the prince.

The prince said, "Then put on your nightshirt and go to bed. I'm tired."

When Darius was tired, they both slept. Dare lived his life around Darius's routine.

He slipped into the dark dressing room adjacent to the closet, taking a single candle with him, and undressed in the shadowy silence.

When he was in his silk nightshirt, he made sure to carefully take off the crown and rings and put them away in the red velvet jewelry box set on a fancy, carved table containing brushes, shaving equipment, bowls, and combs. He kept on only his silver cuff, which belonged to him.

When he came out of the closet, the prince was already in his cushioned, silky bed, propped on pillows and naked from the waist up. His clothing was strewn about the room. He looked up from the book he was paging through and said, "Pick those up, would you, and put them out for the maid."

Dare gathered up the tossed about clothing and put them with the other garments he had worn, all folded neatly into a basket. Then he placed it in the hall for the morning maid to take to the laundress.

He returned to the chamber, noting the prince had put his book away and pinched the candles out. He settled into his floor-mat at the foot of Darius's bed. Only one candle remained burning by the door in the sidewall that led to the water closet where the chamber pot was.

He could easily admit he had it good. After his mother, who was one of the king's trusted servants, had died, he'd been brought to the prince's rooms to live with him and be his companion. Things could have been much worse for him. Instead, he had blankets, pillows and his own cushioned mattress. He was warm, fed and healthy. He had tutors in language, reading, math and philosophy, as well as lessons in history, which Darius so detested.

They'd had years of tactics lessons from a strict sword-master neither of them could ever please. And they'd both learned how to ride together, though Darius hated horses, and these last few years had grown to hate even going outdoors.

He heard Darius shift in the bed above him.

For a moment his heart raced, as he knew what was to come. But along with the anxiety, his body heated.

"Footstool, come up here."

Dare climbed out of his bed and came alongside the bigger one, looking down. In the dim, single-candle light he could just make out the prince's features, dark hair scattered over one eye and pressed against his hot cheek, eyes glistening dark, chin up, bare chest moving up and down a little faster than normal.

He'd pushed the covers all the way down and lay naked on his white sheets. His body was lean and hard, slightly paler than Dare's, ironically softer on the outside than the inside.

"Footstool." A whisper. "Footstool. You have to do what I say because you're mine."

Technically, Darius was right. If Dare disobeyed orders from any royal he served, he could be punished. Darius had proven this reality with the whippings, though they rarely happened. Darius had threatened Dare with punishment for years, but the discipline had never gone further than private, minor whippings.

Darius also had the right to do worse. Dare had been threatened with being thrown in the dungeon for a day. Or, there was the worst case scenario—and it happened when insane men became kings—he could be executed.

The dungeon, a public whipping, or an execution had to be ordered by the king. Dare knew that probably would not happen since Darius did not speak much to his father, unless commanded into meetings with him.

When they were very young and Dare displeased him, Darius used his fists to show displeasure. Or wrestled Dare to the floor and held him in tight, painful positions until Dare begged him to stop.

The king never interfered. If he saw them tussling, he always said, "Let the boys work it out themselves."

But there was no working anything out. Dare was the inferior. He always gave in. If he ever harmed the prince in any severe way, the king would no doubt retaliate. And Darius would not stoop to protect him.

It was easy to just go along with Darius in whatever he wanted, and it generally wasn't difficult to please him. Darius was a simple boy, an unhappy boy.

Dare might have been in the servile position, but he was not as miserable as the broody prince. Life was not a dark place for Dare and he knew he'd been dealt the better hand in life. Darius wanted to feel superior, so he wanted Dare to play the footstool. He wanted someone to let him win at games, do his homework because he could not function on his own to feel good about himself.

For all that, it meant nothing for Dare to give in to the prince's needs. He was all the prince had.

This bed play behavior, however, was new for them. They'd only started this year. The first time had been a debacle. Darius had been so excited, almost unable to tell Dare what he wanted. To *order* Dare. And Dare had been half-afraid but also half-curious. It had lasted only seconds because as soon as Dare's lips had touched Darius's cock, the prince spilled.

Darius had cursed him and told him, "Any whore would have been better than you, Footstool!"

Still, after that, once or twice a week, he began asking Dare to come into his bed.

Without a word, Dare bent his knees and pressed them into the softness of the bed, kneeling by Darius's side. His nightshirt rode up his thighs, a gentle caress. He was hard now, too, just looking at the prince.

And even though he hated him, the body of the prince was pleasing. And perhaps, too, he pitied him. He had come to realize Darius could not help how he was. A miserable, dark soul who hated his own existence and could see nothing good or bright or pretty about the world. He had no one. No one but Dare.

Dare bent down. Darius let out a soft hiss.

He took the prince's stiff cock between his lips and sucked, tasting the bitter salt of it, feeling it jump as he slid his mouth up and down the length.

As he performed this function, his mind wandered to his memory of the view outside the chamber window. One day he thought he might see more of the world, but he was careful not to get his hopes up.

He closed his eyes and saw blue waters, green fields and tree-lined mountains beyond which lay a world of kingdoms and people. He understood that the world was vibrant, that life could thunder inside your chest with vitality or struggle, but either way you could not deny it. The act he was doing, giving pleasure to another, contributed to it.

Darius may have been a bitter, troubled ass, spoiled and mean, but he tasted of a repressed need to fly, slightly sweet, and he trembled for it. It was the only time in their entire companionship that Dare saw him let go of the mental armor he shrouded himself in.

On the outside, the prince was not ugly. The skin of his hips and thighs held a supple warmth where Dare touched him. His muscles were lean, spare, nice to touch. His cock was well-formed, not too big, and actually pretty to look at.

Dare liked boys. A lot. And had known this since he was about twelve. It did not surprise him that this chore made his own body heat as well. It excited him that Darius was excited. He tried not to wish for more.

Just before Darius came, his whole body tensed. Dare felt the balls draw up tight. Heard the breaths come faster, the groans increase in volume.

"Oh, oh, suck hard!"

He smiled and obeyed, and Darius shot into his mouth. Dare teased him gently with his tongue until the organ softened.

18

Darius sat up, saying, "Better than a whore, you are."

Dare shrugged off the insult part of that statement and took it as the best compliment Darius could manage.

"I know you like boys. You like it." Darius reached out and lifted Dare's nightshirt. "Show me."

He always did, ready to obey in this.

Darius said, "You look fucking ready to shoot. Do it."

Dare always did that, too, kneeling by his side, using his own hand, for Darius would never allow himself to actually show affection, to touch him.

Dare stroked himself slowly, knowing that in the thin, single light of the half-burnt candle, Darius could see enough, that the shadows gave them both a little anonymity, but the play of wavering gold-brown light revealed details that brought them both to a sensuous state of arousal.

His cock felt heavy and ready. He wouldn't last long.

Darius hissed, said, "Go faster."

Dare milked himself, feeling the tip of his cock get hotter, his balls tingle, and then the heat exploded through him. He sprayed Darius on the chest. Darius liked it and wordlessly rubbed the semen into his skin.

Dare saw the prince was hard again. That was normal. He bent again to lick him. Stroke him.

When Darius was ready again, he grabbed Dare by the shoulders, pulling him up tight so that his cock pushed against Dare's stomach under his rucked-up nightshirt. He thrust over and over, coming hard.

For a moment, Dare lay against him. They were both breathing hard. The sweat of their lower bodies mingled with their spend. Dare allowed himself to float on the warmth of the embrace. It would only last seconds, so he made them count, pressing his lips to Darius's silken shoulder.

When Darius's breathing quieted, he pushed hard at Dare, saying, as usual, "Off, Footstool. Get off! I have to sleep now or it'll be all your fault if I fall asleep in front of the tutor tomorrow."

That reminded Dare that he had homework to finish for Darius. "I'll get up early and complete your report."

"Yeah, do that. I don't care." He yawned. "You always do, Footstool. Know-it-all."

Dare went back to his own little bed on the floor. He pulled the covers up and turned onto his side, staring at the candle by the far door. It seemed everything about the night was breathing, living.

But something was missing. The prince would never love him. Love. Why did he think he even needed something like that? It was ridiculous. He was a servant and always would be.

But somewhere out in the world he wondered if there was someone like him, thinking as he did at this very moment, that out beyond the walls and lands of a farm or city or castle, the twin to his heart waited to be found.

Chapter Three

Dare slouched against the wall waiting for Darius's meeting with his father to end. He watched the oil lamps flicker in the empty corridor, making eerie shadows on the stone walls.

He wanted to sit, badly, but had been told to stand and wait. Fidgeting from foot to foot, yawning often, he wished for a window, or a book, or a wooden puzzle to solve. Anything but this.

His head lolled, and he thumped the back of it against the hard rock wall over and over until it felt slightly bruised. For a while he jogged in place, counting steps until he lost track of the numbers. He recited poems and songs. Waiting was one of his more exhausting chores.

At long last, the king's parlor door cracked open. He heard voices raised. Darius's was loudest, the king merely sounding annoyed. Darius strode into the hall, fists bunched, brows narrowed, eyes mere slits.

Dare stood up straight and came up alongside him as they made their way down the hall toward their school-room. They were already late meeting their history tutor.

When they got to the school-room door, Darius kept walking past it until they were in the private, east gardens surrounded by lemon and orange trees, the air perfumed with the pollens of locust blossoms, primrose, oleander and orchid.

This was about the furthest Darius ventured outside anymore unless ordered by the king. For most public functions beyond the castle doors, Dare took his place.

Darius led them to his favorite bench inscribed with the name: *Coralie.* The queen's name. She had died giving birth to

Darius. Dare's own mother had died, too, but he'd been five at the time. At least he'd gotten to meet her. Darius had never met his mother.

"Footstool, kneel." Darius's voice came more harsh than cold today.

Dare knelt before the bench and Darius put his feet up onto his back none too gently. Dare felt his vest pull tight at his ribs.

"I could scream right now," the prince said.

"Why?" He gazed at the dusty ground where a loose flower petal, pink-edged, flittered from his breath.

"My father wants to send me away."

"What?"

"Yes. It seems that drama last night with the Shastan delegation was more serious than you could have known. Fuck! I hate him!"

"It was worse than an insult, then."

"Don't be stupid, Footstool. Of course it was! My father wants to declare war on Shastan right away. I'll be safer at the summer chateau, he told me. Well out of the way and surrounded by guards. We're to leave in a fortnight."

"What happened to make the king so angry?" Dare asked.

Darius chuckled coldly. "The delegates wanted to forge a peaceful union between our countries. They made an outrageous suggestion as to how to bring about peace."

"What was it?"

"Marry me off to the Shastan prince."

"The prince?"

"There are no princesses of Shastan right now. So yes, it would be the Crown Prince Malory I would wed. It's a joke. And my father had them thrown out on their asses."

"Would you have even considered it?" Dare asked.

"A marriage? To a barbarian? And a man? *Never!*"

"Well, maybe he's handsome."

"You'd like that, Footstool, wouldn't you!" Darius made a spitting noise.

Dare remained silent. The things they'd done in the late, dark nights. The pleasures Darius could not deny. Even though Darius taunted and teased a few servant girls, he obviously had few objections to men as well. But it was not Dare's position to point that out.

"I don't want to leave here."

Now Darius pouted, pushing his left heel into Dare's ribs.

"But if there must be war, the king is right. You'll be safer," Dare said. He could practically hear Darius glaring.

Nothing would satisfy Darius. Ever. War. No War. Safe. Unsafe. Moving. Never moving. All of life's choices were to be despised.

A low wind moved through the tops of the trees and a soft mist wafted over them, cooling the warmth of the day. Dare smelled green in that breeze, and high skies of freshness. The dank, damp scent of the castle, of burning wax and kitchen smells did not follow them out here. Soon they would be traveling in all that springtime splendor.

Dare's feet itched with a need to get going on their journey. His whole body ached to see the beauties of the outside world. Their whole lives, he and Darius had never ventured far from the castle walls.

They stayed silent for a while.

"Okay, Footstool."

When he was allowed to stand, he saw that Darius's hair sparkled from the mist, as if diamonds had caught themselves in the dark locks. Dare knew his own hair looked almost exactly the same.

The prince had been called handsome, as Dare often was by guards and maids alike. Born to privilege, Darius could have been amazing in so many ways, if not for the constant smirk of the lips. If not for the empty dark of his eyes and his distaste for social gatherings.

Petals spilled across their path: peach-pink, blood, saffron. Green leaves flickered, edged in silver from dappled sunlight making its way through lush growths. Darius picked a bundle of fresh grapes as they walked, but did not offer Dare any, or say that he could pick some, too.

Dare didn't care. The garden made him dreamy. Letting down his guard, he said, "Sometimes I wish I could sleep out here in the summertime, look for the stars."

"That's stupid," Darius said. "And wishing is for tiny children and drooling morons."

"I don't know," Dare ventured.

"You don't? You get hopes up only to have them dashed. Is that smart?"

Dare shrugged.

"Look at me, Footstool," Darius commanded.

They stopped walking. Dare faced his prince. Their eyes met, hollow cold to wide warmth.

"Do you trust me?" Darius asked.

Dare did not answer. He could not. For honesty would insult the prince, and lying, saying he did trust him, would only make Darius laugh and despise him more.

As if out of nowhere, Darius's hand flew up and he smacked Dare hard across the cheek. "There's your answer. A life of wishing. Trust. A fool's errand."

The pain swam through his cheek warming his eyes. Dare stood his ground even as his vision went hazy with tears.

Darius's mouth, shaped into a cruel curl of permanent disgust, widened in a strange smile. "You're lucky you have me around to keep you in place. You need me."

Dare could only swallow and nod. He followed the prince back into the shadows.

*

24

As the days grew closer to the date they would leave for the summer chateau, Darius's behavior became even more erratic and mean. He would often pinch Dare on the arms, the buttocks, and the chest for no reason. He had major tantrums, and threw his belongings about the room, broke things, yelled profanities, screamed at the top of his lungs until he was breathless.

Dare must've cleaned the chamber no less than five times, sweeping, putting things back where they belonged, sending ripped clothing to the maids for repair.

Darius avoided all his tutors. Sometimes Dare went to class alone, but mostly he stayed with Darius waiting for his command, suffering alongside him, forced to listen to his ravings about not wanting to leave the castle. Ever.

The king paid them a rare visit, entering the prince's chambers with a silent, dark-clad guard at his back.

Dare had been at his usual place by the window, taking fresh air into his lungs whenever he could, grappling with his worn-out patience. The room was a mess again, bedcovers thrown against the far wall, pillows tossed aside, Dare's own floor-mat turned upside-down. The wax of tipped candles had spilled and dried on the floor. Ruby-studded wine decanters lay in smashed shards about the chamber.

Darius stood in the center of the room as his father entered. He faced his father but his head was down, hands behind his back. His shiny dark locks spilled against his cheeks, hiding half his face. The only time Dare ever saw Darius submit like that was to the king.

In all fairness, the king was imposing. He stood six foot five, and was muscled like an ox. His thick robe made him appear even bigger. He had the same dark glare as Darius, but not quite as uncontrolled or cruel. Craggy lines about his eyes spoke of age, and of grief. His wife, Queen Coralie, had died giving birth to Darius. People said the king still visited her tomb every day, his mourning for her fresh as the day Darius was born.

"What is the meaning of this madcap behavior!" the king demanded as he glanced about the room.

The prince did not move. Nor answer.

The king turned his attention to Dare.

"And you. Part of your job entails seeing to the prince's needs. Keeping him placated. Why are you not doing your duty?"

"Y… Your Highness." He started to stutter, his throat dry. "I… it is simply that the prince is distressed. He does not wish to leave this beautiful castle."

Darius tilted his head, snarling, voice a hiss. "You do not speak for me!"

"Apologies, my lord."

"Then speak for yourself, son," the king replied.

"I don't like the chateau." He nearly spat the words.

"What's not to love about the chateau?" the king asked. "This time of year the willows are green, the lakes are getting warm for swimming, and the kin-trees let loose their seeds like snow."

"It's too small," the prince complained.

"It has fourteen luxurious guest bedrooms. Three levels and a storage dungeon. Twenty-seven balconies, and vast acres of gardens. A full contingent of servants. What is small about that?"

Darius stomped his foot.

"Stop being insolent this instant. You will be safer at the chateau. You are going in three days and that is my order."

"I won't," said Darius.

"You won't what?" The king's low voice came out softer but far from gentle. The tone held a threat Dare never wanted to see played out.

"I won't go! To leave here is even more dangerous. To travel through the forests—"

"You will have a full guard," the king said.

"I don't care. I'm not going."

"I will drag you onto your horse, if that's what it will take."

Now Darius looked up, chin high "You'll have to tie me to her, then."

"Do not provoke me, young one!"

"There are bandits and thieves in the forest hungry for royalty to hold hostage for ransom!"

"Then let Dare ride as your substitute in full princely regalia. That is what I gave him to you for, to see that you are safe, to do your bidding. Make him ride in the lead."

"I will gladly do it to please the prince." Dare spoke up quickly.

"See?" The king reached out and patted Darius none too lightly on the shoulder. "It's settled then."

Darius flinched at the touch.

The king circled around him slowly, taking in the broken and torn items strewn all over the floor. He met Dare's eyes briefly, and then headed for the door.

"No more outbursts! And get this place cleaned up."

"Yes, Your Highness," said Dare.

When the door closed, Darius let out an anguished growl. "Yes, Your Highness." He mimicked Dare's tone perfectly. He went to him and punched him in the chest. "Kiss-up!"

"I'm on your side," Dare started to protest. Another punch to his chest stopped him.

"Well, go ahead and fucking clean all this up."

"Yes, my lord."

Dare began to gather the torn clothing and put it in a basket. He watched out the corner of his eye as Darius went to the foot of his bed and sat. Head down, he rubbed at his face angrily.

Dare suppressed a sigh, and continued to clean.

Darius kicked at a pillow by his foot, sending it flying. "I don't want to go!"

"Why?" Dare had asked him this question before, never getting an answer.

Darius said, "This is my room. These are my things. I'm comfortable here."

Dare nodded. "Me, too." That was when he realized that Darius was actually afraid. He'd never been anywhere much further than a couple miles outside Castle Brookfall's walls.

Darius did not respond. Instead, he curled up on his bed, facing away from Dare, and stayed that way for the better part of the afternoon.

Dare finished his tidying, then left him to sleep. He went down to the kitchens to order them a dinner of all of Darius's favorite foods. It was the kindest thing he could think of to do. Darius did not deserve him.

Chapter Four

In the distance, dawn peeked like gilt brocade over the horizon. Westward, the falls crashed, white and frothy. The first day of their journey, they would make their way down to the narrow valley past the great falls. Dare looked forward to it. The courtyard was a whirlwind of servants, stable-boys, trainers and guards. And horses.

Dew sprinkled the horses' manes. The prince's horse was an all-black mare, stronger than most of the other horses, and more beautiful. Darius had had her since he was nine. He'd named her Midnight. One of the few astute things Dare had seen Darius do.

Midnight was the horse Dare rode now.

He wore a deep red velvet coat, a favorite of Darius's, and a white shirt underneath with a gold vest embroidered elaborately with trees and birds. He had on black wool trousers, and knee-high, black leather boots. The crown in his dark hair was gold-leaf and simple, good for traveling as it wasn't going to fall off if the horses trotted rough roads.

Darius insisted that Dare wear his princely rings and an emerald necklace. The stone was the size of an egg, and a little heavy for travel, not to mention tempting to thieves, but Darius said Dare wouldn't look like a prince if he didn't dress and accessorize for the part.

Darius wore the gray and black of servant attire, with a muffin cap on his head to hide his looks. He wore Darius's brown leather boots. The two of them were the same size pretty much all over, even their feet. Darius rode Dare's sweet gray mare, Sylph, and she tolerated him well.

When Dare wore the prince's clothes, he felt himself change inside. Though all of it was a sham, a sense of importance surrounded him. He held his head high and his upper body stiff and tall on the big horse. Somehow, knowing he looked good, looked the part, influenced how he felt about himself.

A soft wind blew Dare's hair back from the leaf crown, feathering it. Everything sparkled as the dawn filled the world with its sprinkling of lavender, gold and muted blue light. Everything was ready. The journey would take three days.

It was strange when the king did not see them off. He cared enough to send his son away for safety, but not enough to say good-bye.

The gates opened that led to the bridge over the chasm. Two guards, Bron and Thos, took the lead. Dare rode behind them. Another group of guards followed. Then came the servants, including Darius, who looked sullen astride Sylph. But Sylph was an even-tempered creature, and did not seem bothered.

Though Dare lived a life of pretending all the time—pretending he liked and admired the prince, constantly trying to convince himself he was lucky to live a sheltered and luxurious life with a prince—he actually reveled in playing the part of the prince.

And, in a set up like this, for the whole day, Dare did not have to worry about Darius. The prince was far enough behind him that he couldn't indulge him in his depressing viewpoints, and Dare did not have to put up with his pinching and punching, and his shallow insults. He did not have look at the ugly and permanent snarl that was his mouth.

The iron bridge that crossed the chasm and separated the castle from the farmlands surrounding it had been built before the castle was erected. It seemed older than time itself, but withstood the centuries with solid craftsmanship. Only the wooden planks across the flooring had been replaced. Every decade or so, when the wood started to rot, workers came out and nailed new boards in place.

The horses' hooves clomped across the bridge making so much noise it echoed in staccato beats across the narrow valley.

It seemed to take forever for the entire train of travelers to finish crossing the bridge, but finally all were moving more comfortably along the softer earth of the fields, and Dare delighted in the now lightening, boundless blue skies, the scent of new alfalfa, and the sight of an endless horizon.

Darius was no doubt hating it all, but Dare didn't have to think about that.

Midnight wanted to trot, go faster. Dare reined her in to a smooth, fast walk. He glided on the path between the fields, and Dare was so happy for the new experience he couldn't keep the huge smile off his face.

After they crossed a few miles of meadows, they took a single file path down into the narrow valley. The base of the mountain shadowed them. Dare could look back and see the castle up on the great hill opposite the falls. It sported many levels and towers covered with gray lichen and old yellow moss, aged but beautiful against its own purple shadow and blue sky above. Birds took off and landed on the roofs of the topmost towers.

Dare thought the sound of the falls might spook the horses, but they stayed calm through the mists and the roar of water, moving along the damp ground, their bodies shining.

After a couple of hours, the valley widened to rocky outcroppings and stunted trees. At midday, they stopped for a meal and let the horses graze.

Darius found Dare and sat beside him to eat his bread and cheese. He said snidely, "You look far too happy to be impersonating me."

"I like the outdoors."

"Well, I don't. It makes me itchy and tired. And you are supposed to be me. So stop enjoying yourself!"

It was one of the most ridiculous things Dare had ever heard Darius say—and Darius had said a lot of stupid things—and he could not suppress a quiet chuckle.

Darius said, "Oh shut up."

They moved on through the afternoon as the light grew ancient and orange toward sunset. Giant boulders old as time itself surrounded them, along with a few spindly trees. Many miles away, they still had the Great Forest to traverse. Two more days and they'd be at the chateau.

The prince's guard erected a large tent for Darius and Dare to share. More tents went up. Fire rings glowed. The cook who'd come along made a stew from dried meats and vegetables.

Out in the open air, the stew was the best thing Dare had ever tasted. He took second helpings as Darius scowled and complained that his was cold, moving off to eat in the tent.

Later, on his silken palace that he slept on to keep up the illusion that he was the prince, Dare slept soundly, his dreams like cool mist against the sides of his mind.

*

Just as the dawn sent ribbons of golden light into the air, the party, fed on a quick breakfast of hot bread and porridge, started out again.

As the day wore on, the light grew watery and pale. The horses were more skittish than usual. It was not hot but the sun seemed to sear everything in their path—rocks, twisted trees, cliff faces—to yellow, gray and burnt green. The flowers were covered in dust. Instead of spring, it felt like autumn.

Dare looked forward to the Great Forest, hoping for more muted tones of purples, grays and blues. To feel the thick green air of rivers again.

32

Finally, they came over a rise and Dare saw, in the distance, a sweeping greenness move up the land to the mountains. Ahead was the first line of trees.

Already, they were half-way to the chateau. He couldn't wait to explore a new place.

They stopped at the first line of trees to eat lunch. The horses were still nervous but calmed as they grazed.

Deep into the trees, Dare saw spears of sunlight like crystal shards stabbing through the high branches. The shade looked cool. He could not yet hear the river, but he could smell it, wet-moss and rain. Pink and violet flowers bloomed over the ground. Bees hummed. Birds laughed.

Servants and guards wandered about relieving themselves, eating, organizing their packs for the rest of the journey. The glade they were in was peaceful.

Dare closed his eyes and drifted. The ground was cool against his back and buttocks. He could hear Darius at his side, fidgeting, unhappy. But not even that could disturb his contentment.

He did not know how long he dozed, but something in the air changed, and he sat up, blinking to see the prince's guardsmen gathering in formation, and heard the chime of metal on metal as swords were drawn.

Abruptly, he stood. "What's happening?"

Darius, already standing, shaded his eyes with his hand. "Horses. Strangers. Looks like a lot of them."

Dare looked in the same direction, seeing a band of riders heading their way through a barren field to the right, an ocher dust cloud following behind them. It looked as if they had come from the forest high on the ridge.

"I told you," Darius began. "We should never have left the castle. My father is a stupid, *stupid* man. Fuck! This isn't good."

"We have two dozen guards," Dare said calmly. But his heart thumped in his chest. His throat tightened.

When the horde got closer, they slowed. A single rider approached their party, dressed in a black guard's uniform and sable cloak. The blue unicorn crest of Shastan was stamped on the guard's breastplate, and on the front metal plate his horse wore. Behind that rider looked to be more than twenty men, maybe thirty, all dressed the same.

Dare could not see the lead guardsman's entire face. He wore a gray metal helm that curved downward over the nose, revealing only the eyes. The sides of the helm pressed against the jaws and cheeks and fastened just under the chin, framing full pink lips.

The prince's own guards wore similar helms, but less elaborate. And their entire faces showed. Their blackbird crest was neatly etched into their breastplates. All the Brookfall men had their swords out.

Thos stepped to the front of the group as the rider stopped about ten paces away.

"Why do you approach?" asked Thos.

The rider sat still as a sculpture upon his mount. After an intimidating moment, his head turned slightly and his eyes met Dare's.

"What have we here? The crown prince of Brookfall?"

"You shall retreat at once!" Thos shouted. He stomped one foot and held his sword arm out with the weapon still facing the ground.

Not far away, the grazing horses whickered, lifted their elegant heads and flicked their long tails. They sensed the threat, but went back to their grazing, some heading slowly away.

Without their horses, the Brookfall men were at a disadvantage.

At Dare's side, Darius whispered, "Fuck!"

The rider swept his gaze over the entire party, two dozen guards, six servants including Darius, and Dare. He said nothing.

"Retreat now or this will be seen as an act of aggression!" Thos tossed his head back. His helm gave a low clink.

"Aggression? Us? But, my good sir, rumors abound. Brookfall is to declare war upon Shastan."

"There is no war declared," Thos argued.

Dare knew he spoke the truth. The king would wait until his son was confirmed safe before he did that.

"Not yet. And we cannot afford for that to ever happen now, can we?"

Thos seemed not to know what to say to that. The other guards shifted. Dare smelled the sourness of fear and aggression breaking over them as they began to sweat under their cloaks.

Finally, Thos found his voice. "You will leave us in peace."

"Ah, but there is no peace between us. Are you escorting the prince to a safe locale?"

When Thos did not answer right away, the rider continued. "I think you are. That could be seen as an act of war to some with suspicious natures. Therefore, I have a proposition. If you agree, there will be peace, I assure you." His horse danced a bit, then quieted.

"What proposition?" Thos's voice held a tense note of accusation.

"It's a simple request, actually. Hand the prince over to us and we shall leave."

"What?" Insulted, Thos took a threatening step forward.

"This proposal had been given to your king only two weeks ago to ensure peace between our countries. He rejected it. With no small amount of anger, I might add."

"Of course His Highness, our High King of Brookfall would never give his son over as a hostage to the likes of you!" Thos replied.

"He was not to be a hostage, but to wed the Shastan heir."

"The king of Shastan has no daughters!"

"This is true. He would wed the crown prince, of course. It is lawful for two princes of conflicted realms to marry to solidify peace treaties between their countries. This is common courtesy between kingdoms to ensure trust and loyalty and keep the peace. But your king would not have it."

"But—but—" Thos puffed out a breath. "The crown prince is too young to wed."

"A lie. But never mind. You are forgiven. Hand him over and no harm will come to anyone. The prince Darius will be kept well and safe in our hands, and war shall be averted. But should your king declare war, the prince's life will be forfeit."

"*Now* you lie! That is a hostage situation."

"Oh, things have changed since your king insulted and threatened our country. And the proposition has changed to suit the times. Yes, he will now be a hostage. Much to the relief of the crown prince of Shastan, I'm sure, for who would ever wish to wed a Brookfall monster?"

Thos stomped his foot again. "You will take the crown prince of Brookfall over my dead body!"

Dare started at the statement. Had Thos forgotten *he* was posing as the prince? They could turn him over and the prince would still be safe.

"Then we will do just that," the rider replied, as unconcerned as if he were discussing trade routes and when the next shipments of grain might be expected.

Dare stepped forward. "Wait!"

But the rider had already made a wave and a hand signal. He did not see or hear him.

Dare shouted louder. "Wait!"

But men were shouting, and the Shastan guard was moving forward. The Brookfall guards began to shout as well.

36

Cloaks were thrown to the ground, swords wielded and ready.

"I'll go with them! I'll go!"

No one heard Dare except Darius, who stood wide-eyed and scowling at the entire fiasco. Then he laughed and said, "They're really going to fight over *you*."

"Stop them!" Dare cried. "This isn't funny!"

But already Thos and the rider's swords clashed in the crisp air, and the horses of the Brookfall guards were running away.

"Too late!" Darius grabbed Dare and pulled him back from the melee. The other servants were already running, but Shastan guards ran them down.

The first to fall was the cook, and as Dare watched, the cook's head flew up in an arc of red, and disappeared in thick grass.

Dare had never seen anyone killed before. Not even an execution.

"Darius?"

Darius froze. His hands clutched tighter to Dare's shoulder and arm.

Seeing he, too, was in shock, Dare said, "Come with me. Run!"

Together, they took off toward the line of trees heading for the heavier shadows and the forest. A forest they knew nothing about.

The meadow gave way to trees, and they crashed through thick undergrowth dotted in little white, star-shaped flowers. Their perfume dusted their coats and Dare thought, *It's sweet. Even among terrible things, so sweet.*

In his terror, every detail became clear to him. The little starflowers, the way their two bodies squashed the blooms as they broke through the bushy growth. The change of temperature to cool silence as they came into the shadows of bigger trees. The scent of loam and moss and bark filling their lungs.

Dare was aware of every breath Darius took. How he hissed "fuck fuck fuck" under his breath as they ran still clutched together. How his face had gone pale, almost green, his hair slicked and shining with the sweat of panic.

The path before them was filled with broken branches and sticks. Wildflower patches grew in the areas where sunlight broke through and pooled in brilliant flashes.

Muffled yells and crunching footsteps sounded behind them.

Dare pulled Darius along, quickening their pace. They leapt over bushes, rocks and roots. Dare looked around frantically for any place they might be able to get out of sight, but the trees, though thick, did not offer cover, and there were no cliffs to jump, no rivers to swim. Not yet.

"Run faster," he breathed, and felt Darius step it up.

They flew as only two eighteen year old boys could, past low hanging branches that tried to hook their hair and coats, leaping logs, crushing foliage.

Dare could not afford to lose any momentum looking behind them to see how close their pursuers were. He dodged between trees so fast he nearly pulled Darius off-balance. But Darius, still grumbling curses, kept up. Their way cleared a little and they sprinted faster.

Right into the hands of two Shastan guards.

Chapter Five

Dare hit his pursuer so hard with his body that he nearly knocked them both to the forest floor. An echoing grunt came from Darius but he could not see him. He could hear him, though, yelling now as loud as a storm, pissed as could be.

"Hands off, you oaf! Fucker! Get off me!"

Dare struggled hard, crying out, but his captor quickly got his arms in a strong grip, turned him, and wrenched them behind his back. He kicked and half-fell, pulling as hard as he could.

A loud scream filled the air, growing in pitch, turning his blood to ice. He went limp in the arms of the Shastan guard and turned his head in time to see a silver spike come up and out of the back of Darius's servant coat. A circle of red began to form around the blade.

Dare fell forward. "No, no, no, no!"

His captor still held his arms, but loosened his grip so he could kneel. The other guard held Darius aloft on his sword for a moment before finally pulling it out with a slick and horrible sound. Darius slumped, then fell forward with a faint groan.

Dare reached out and caught him.

He heard the guard say, "Don't hurt the prince, damn it!" as he struggled to remain close to Darius.

"No, you can't—This isn't—No, no no," Dare heard himself say. His arms were released. Immediately, he put them around Darius, holding him up, shoulder butting into his chest, and looked at his face.

Darius glanced up, eyebrow rising as if in surprise. "Dare?"

He couldn't even think. He put his hand up to Darius's cheek. "It's not that bad. It's all right."

"Oh, fuck, it hurts. It hurts."

Dare cupped his face with one hand, and held him with his arm around his upper back tight to his chest. He felt the thundering heartbeat of fear, and ignored the blood that pooled on the grass, on his sleeve, and in his lap beneath Darius's back.

"You'll be fine," Dare lied. "It's not as bad as it seems. You're fine." He brought his forehead down to touch the top of Darius's head.

"You always lie to me, Footstool."

"I—never-- "

"I'm glad. Glad I'm dying. It's stupid. Everything is stupid. My father—" Tears spilled over his cheeks but he seemed not to notice. His breathing grew faster, his voice now a whisper. "And you'll die, too. You'll see. They think you're the prince now," he murmured into Dare's chest. "Well, be me. I don't care. But you'll find out what it's like. Everything will go wrong for you. You'll see."

The guards were mumbling to each other. They hadn't heard.

Dare smelled the metallic salts of Darius's life draining away. So much blood. His sleeve was soaked. His thigh. His own tears tasted bitter as they dripped onto his lips and spilled over to his chin and into Darius's face.
He had never liked Darius, but they'd grown up together. There was *something* between them, even if only a thin thread of brotherhood.

He did not want him to die. Not like this.

The hollow eyes became even more hazed. The breathing more shallow until the prince's body jerked twice and was still. No breath remained.

Without warning, he began to weep so hard he couldn't breathe. He felt one of the guards pulling him up. "Come along," he heard.

He gasped. "You killed him and he wasn't even armed."

"You were all warned."

"No—"

Dare's body shook with sobs as he was dragged through the woods and back into the meadow. Blinking in the clearer sunlight, he tried to catch his breath and look around. But things only got worse.

All the men of the prince's guard were dead in the field, as well as all the servants. And there was so much blood.

More tears spilled down his cheeks. He felt his hands grasped and pulled behind his back again, and a something knotting his wrists together. He fell to his knees, head bowed, and gasped for breath.

He heard voices around him but not what they were saying. Everything was like a dream, distant, echoing, senseless. Long, pale green grasses bent against his thighs. He saw a black beetle no bigger than his pinky fingernail crawl into a thicker mass of green.

A hand cupped him under the arm and yanked him. "Up, Prince!"

His legs trembled. He'd quieted now, numb and silent. He almost could not stand. He looked down at himself, soaked with fresh blood, grass sticking to his trousers--the prince's trousers made of wool, soft and pliant, and above them the brocade on the prince's vest, the red velvet of the prince's coat. The prince's rings flashed in the sad light.

The guard who had clasped his upper arm said, "You will come with us to Shastan and you will not make trouble. Do you understand?"

Dare took a deep breath, swallowed and nodded.

He pulled Dare hard to face the meadow. "Now," said the guard, "which one of these were you riding?"

Dare looked up to see that some of the horses had not run and were still peacefully grazing, rumps facing them. Midnight stood among them, well-trained, loyal. He could not see Sylph, who must have run into the woods.

"The black one," he whispered. "Midnight."

*

His system in shock, his senses focused on faraway things. He heard the wild grasses shuffle and hum in the breeze. As he rode, a flock of geese called overhead. Insects flew up at their passing, iridescent-winged, free. The sun slashed its white light in shards all through the trees, making cobbled shadows on the ground before them, a ghost road through the forest.

Dare's hands were tied behind his back, but he could smell the mossy ecstasy of the river and hear secret and hidden falls. His tears dried tight and sticky on his cheeks, and blood soaked the sleeves of Darius's beautiful red coat staining them brown. Still the birds sang.

The odd thing was, though Darius had been troubled, he'd been right about everything. The world might be a beautiful backdrop, but it was merely the fancy plate upon which horror was eventually served, for no goodness lasted forever, no happiness, no peace.

The enemy guard beside Dare reached across their two horses and smacked him on the shoulder. Dare was so used to being hit, he barely felt it.

"If you fall off that horse, you will be dragged all the way to Shastan. Three days. You won't survive it."

Clenching his tied wrists against his lower back, he sat up straighter and blinked against the puffs of dirt, sticks and flower petals kicked up by the horses' hooves.

He was a prince now. He must act the part better than he ever had. His life depended on it.

Chapter Six

"Take this and be glad." The Shastan guard had tied Dare to a tree just before dusk, leaving his right hand free and enough room for his reclining body to turn a little in the dirt if he had to pee. The hemp rope wrapped several times around his waist, then several times about the tree, with slack in-between. He wasn't uncomfortable. He could even curl up on his side if he wanted to.

The guard handed him a wooden bowl and spoon. Dare took the bowl with trembling fingers.

The others called this guard Hoop. His fingernails were bitten to the quick in black lines, and his light hair was already thinning, though he looked no more than thirty. He was gruff and ungentle but not mean. Dare had been treated worse by Darius. So far.

Still in shock, his stomach ached as if it were filled with stones. He didn't want the stew, but steam from the bowl rose bluish in the firelight and filled him with a scent of fresh potatoes, carrots and what smelled like rabbit. His stomach clenched and released and when he inhaled again his body said, *yes.*

He lifted the spoon to his lips, tasted, and swallowed a bit of salty gravy. His body swooned and he ate the stew as quickly as he could shovel it in, then set the bowl aside.

Too fast. His belly felt like rocks again.

He leaned his head back on the bark of the tree, listening to the voices of the men, three dozen in all. In the fight they'd lost one man and one horse. One more man was wounded. The wounded man lay in a tent not far off and Dare heard the others say he would live.

Dare thought back on his own party. All of them dead. They hadn't had a chance, ambushed as they were. Out-numbered.

The stars started to come out and he could see them wink between the canopy of leaves. Beautiful but comfortless. His eyes grew hot. He shut them tight, refusing to cry. He'd already shed too many tears today.

He could still see the blood pooling beneath Darius, and feel the way his body went limp and light in his arms as he died.

Part of him thought he should consider himself lucky. He was the only survivor. Alive. The Shastans might despise him, but they had not hurt him. It was pure fate. Only because he wore prince's garb had he been spared. They'd wanted Darius, not him.

He did not know how long he could keep up the charade of being Prince Darius, but he had no choice. Darius had even said, "Be me", just before he died. But it had been more of a curse than an order. He'd died just as angry as he had been when alive. He'd died in pain.

Dare took a deep, shaky breath.

He'd substituted for the prince on so many public occasions at the castle it felt natural. He'd lived with the prince since he was a little boy, was taught by the same tutors, was brought up with the same manners and attire. He knew what a prince expected from his servants, what protocols to follow both in public and private. And he knew Darius well. It would be like breathing for him to keep playing the role. The only thing he did not mirror well was the prince's bullying nature.

But these strangers—these Shastans—had never met Prince Darius. They had only heard rumors of Darius's questionable personality. Dare felt safe in the thought that he could be himself and act the princely part and no one would be the wiser. And if he ever returned to Castle Brookfall, he would deal with the repercussions of impersonation then.

Somewhere nearby, he heard Midnight whicker. He could not see the horses from where he was tied, but he was glad they had all survived. One by one, they'd all been rounded up. Midnight was his now, and he would take responsibility for her. If allowed.

The night deepened.

Dare's body shook with exhaustion but he could not sleep. Two guards stayed awake the first half of the night, softly conversing and keeping an eye on him. He tried to ignore them. But that wasn't what kept him awake. He could not get the images of death from his mind. The cook and Darius were forefront, for it was them he'd seen killed with his own eyes. But he'd seen the dead bodies of the rest of the guards and servants, and the horror of it all made his heart race.

The images kept him jerking awake all the way to dawn. As soon as he fell into a sounder sleep, the birds of the forest began to sing. Men woke and built up the fires. Made noise.

Dare hid his face behind his one free arm. But it was no use. He felt wrung out. Weak. Sick. Two more days of travel to survive. He could do it. He had to. But then what?

Someone kicked him in the side. Pain radiated throughout his body. Slowly, he sat up.

In the mists, Hoop stood over him. "Your royal ass no longer has the privilege of sleeping in." He held out a bowl.

Dare took it, seeing the hot but lumpy porridge. His stomach rebelled.

"Thank you," he said.

Hoop frowned. "Don't thank me. Thank the king. His orders were that you're not to be harmed. That includes not letting you starve. But don't think I'm ever going to wait on the likes of you. Once we get to Shastan, you're the dungeon-master's problem."

"Dungeon-master?"

Hoop grinned. "Don't worry. He has a gentle side. About one day a year."

Dare gulped. Looked down at his porridge. He was going to be sick but he didn't want Hoop to see. He sat very still and silent.

Finally, the guard walked away.

Dare turned his body and quietly threw up. He buried the mess and the porridge together, then leaned back against the tree feeling cold slick sweat on his brow.

Not long after, Hoop returned for the empty bowl and the spoon. He let Dare up to relieve himself, keeping the end of the rope about his fist as he stood a few feet away. Soon he was mounted on Midnight and the day's journey began.

After a few hours, the forest thinned. The sun against Dare's back and on his dirty coat made him sweat. His head swam. The bloodstained sleeves warmed and gave off a sharp stink. His mouth tasted of sour milk. His stomach rumbled.

He tried not to think. But amidst scenes of slaughter, and still hearing the last heartbeats of Darius as if he still held him in his arms, he kept hearing Hoop's words. *Dungeon-master.*

There was a dungeon at Castle Brookfall. A high brick wall surrounded the area. It was separate from the castle, in another building on the grounds, one that had no windows save little holes near the roof that let in air and light. That building held a prison, and for all of Dare's life it had been off-limits.

Once, when they were about thirteen, before Darius's fear of the outdoors became extreme, Dare and Darius snuck out of the castle before dawn, went around to the far side of the wall, and climbed it. Through the early morning shadows, they saw several milling guardsmen, a couple of acres of barren ground, and the flat, dark building.

Darius told stories as if he knew everything. He said the prison held murderers, thieves, enemy spies, and deserters. Traitors to the king were executed there. Since

Brookfall executions had never been public in his lifetime, Dare had never seen one. But he had seen people taken away never to be heard from again.

Darius told him some criminals were so violent they had to be chained up all the time. Or tortured to keep them sick and weak. Many died before the king could order their executions, and Darius claimed that since they had not received their proper sentencing their spirits could not rest.

The morning they'd peered over the brick wall, Dare had actually hoped to see a ghost. Or even the sound of a scream. But he'd heard nothing. The silence of the place made it even more ominous.

The dungeon-master of Brookfall was particularly frightening. Dare had first seen him as a child. His name was Clove—a heady spice—and whenever Dare attended court with Darius in the throne room, the dungeon-master stood next to the king's dais with a line of other important men of the realm. He was tall with craggy features, and had thin wisps of hair framing a bald pate. His eyes were small, nearly hidden in the deep crevices of his face.

Clove would have been frightful to meet in any venue, but being the dungeon-master made people shiver just to hear his name. And those eyes were so glinting and beady. Dare had a dream once that when those eyes looked at you they somehow marked you for a future in that dungeon.

He shuddered to think of the Shastan dungeon-master. Surely, he'd be worse. And Dare, being an enemy and supposedly a prince would be treated with nothing less than vile loathing and disgust.

"Hey, hey!"

A fist slammed against his arm. Startled, Dare sat upright.

"Are you daft in the head? You're falling right off your horse." Hoop shook his head, his helm clanking.

Dare had not realized he'd canted to one side. He was so tired, though his thoughts churned. He felt half in, half out of his body. As if he floated about a foot above his head.

In his shock, everything around him yesterday had taken on fine detail, as if his eyes had opened wider than ever before. Today the world looked muted, like peeking through thin, shredded silk.

His face felt tight with dirt and dried tears. His hair hung in tangled clumps against his cheeks and forehead. He must look a sight. Surely not like a prince. His mouth was dry, but he didn't dare ask for water.

When they stopped at noon, again he could not eat and buried his food so they would not know. He did finally drink some water, but immediately threw it up.

Back on Midnight, he repressed his groans at the deep aches of his body. But even when the horse walked softly on smooth, flat ground the rocking motion made the world spin. It took all his strength to keep upright. He stared straight ahead, and saw very little but shapes and shades tinged with a red-pink hue.

More than once he caught himself falling forward in the saddle, his face inches from Midnight's glossy, black mane. Darius would have laughed to see him so dopey. He would have teased him mercilessly, and then called him off the horse to go inside and kneel.

He could hear his voice, now, "Footstool. Footstool. What are you thinking? Kneel. Now. You have to do everything I say. Everything."

He blinked hard as he felt himself fall forward again. The world was filled with flowers. He could see all the colors of the rainbow before him, smell the sweet spring fragrances. Everything was so beautiful and he floated through it all. The peacefulness. The serenity.

From a far distance, he heard a shout. Something touched him. Hands maybe. Whispers came into his mind meaning nothing.

48

"Something's wrong…" "The prince is…" "…he breathing?" "…skin like a torch…"

A coolness touched his face. He woke for a moment and wondered how he'd gotten on the ground.

A shadow said, "He can't ride."

Dare tried to protest. Of course he could ride. He tried to move to prove it and his head fell back into dirt and rock as if it weighed more than the world itself. Something was very wrong. Although he'd known it, he had thought maybe it was only shock and that he would snap out of it. But this was something else.

They had a provision wagon where the injured guard had been riding. They put him in it where it was even hotter. Bumpier. He lay on cloth bags of potatoes, onions, flour. Pots and pans hung on the wagon's low wooden sides and banged as the wagon moved, making his ears ring and his head pound. In his dim awareness, he tried to crawl out of his coat, but had no strength. He threw up again. Nothing but bile. And then only dry heaves. He dreamed the wagon was on fire.

*

Something jarred him awake and the flames receded to a blurred, canvas ceiling flapping in the wind. The wagon jerked and shuddered. Dare turned over and buried his face in the cloth of a food bag, smelling the sweet spice of onions. He expected to gag, but instead the scent calmed him. He breathed shallowly, closed his eyes, and tried to relax.

He could not sleep. Not with the bumps of the wheels on the road, and the sway of the rickety cart. He was so hot and wet his body felt as if it had been recently dumped in a steaming bath. His hair stuck to his neck and face. Where he touched the bags, he left damp handprints.

He still could not quite believe Darius was dead. He thought about crying again but no tears would come. His body was dehydrated. His throat sore and dry.

Exhausted, he drew his knees tight to his chest, wrapping his arms about them. Only then did he notice he'd been untied. He figured they knew he wasn't going to get far if he tried anything. He was too sick.

His teeth began to chatter though he was still sweating. He heard groaning and opened his eyes expecting to see someone in there with him, then realized it was his own voice. He could not help the moans. Or stop the shaking of his arms and legs.

He heard Darius say, "What are you going to do now, Footstool? You're doomed."

In his mind he saw the scowling prince lounging beside him, propped on one elbow, dark hair in disarray about his forehead and shoulders. He looked pompous and smug.

"I told you we shouldn't have gone. It wasn't safe. My father should never have trusted we could make this journey."

Dare had the strangest thought. Maybe the king had wanted to get rid of Darius. But no, spoiled or not, he was the heir. The king knew his line must continue. Didn't he?

Well, now Darius was dead. But everyone thought he was alive. How long would it take for word to get to Brookfall that Prince Darius was being held hostage? How long before a peace was negotiated and Dare was released only to return to a disappointed ruler who thought his son was still alive?

He could not even imagine that day. And without Darius to serve, despite the prince's bullying personality, what would he return to? Would Brookfall even be a home to him now? Would the king welcome him, or lash out at him for not being his son, for surviving when everyone else was killed?

When he closed his eyes he saw dark images of hands flailing, grabbing, hitting. He heard loud voices accusing him of impersonating a royal subject, and more voices shouting, "Death! Death!"

Dying was something he had hoped to put off for a long, long time. But now things had changed. The Shastans hated him, and if Brookfall did not make peace, would they execute him?

First things first. He had to survive this horror of a wagon ride. And the accompanying fever.

Chapter Seven

The next day came in a blur. He remembered only flashes of images: A helmed guard, like a man made of metal, carrying him. A bit of starry sky. A dark, tall shadow, high as the moon. Himself moving into that shadow and watching the flickering lights go by as he floated along an alien corridor. Echoing footsteps. Scents of lavender, bitter tea, cold wetness on his hot skin.

He heard moans and cries and decided he was in a dungeon full of rats and horrible tortures, though he could not see. It seemed things burned him at random, and any touch to his body felt sharp and left him aching afterward.

The darkness was the worst. He could not see what was coming. Everything was an anticipation of what might befall him. Pain only. And more pain.

There were accented voices, male and female, but he could never make out what they were saying. He forgot where he was for a while. He did not have the energy to care. If days passed, or weeks, he couldn't know. He had no sense of time.

Finally, one day he opened his eyes and felt the cushion of a bed, a soft pillow under his head. Robed figures brought him tea, and gently propped him up to drink though his head spun.

They were scary at first, bald and genderless, stoic but soft in their gazes. He thought maybe they were his torturers. But they treated him gently.

In their strange kindness, they bathed him, took care of his needs, dressed him, brought him more tea. In dulcet voices, they said, "Be patient. You will be well soon." Or they asked him simple questions. "Do you hurt here?" "Are you hungry?" "Do you wish for another pillow?"

His nightmares of a dungeon, he realized later, had been fever dreams. Put there into his mind at the suggestion of Hoop who'd taunted him about dungeon-masters.

So he'd been sick. Very sick. And still was recovering.

He kept thinking it might have been better if he'd been left to die. Like all the others from Brookfall traveling to the chateau. But unlike Darius, he saw the world as a place he still wanted to be in.

As he took deeper breaths every day toward recovery, he was grateful to be alive.

*

"I came to see what a barbarian prince looks like. Nothing much, I see."

A man stood framed in thin, yellow light from the high window, a lean silhouette. Dare could not make out his features, nor his age. But the voice, despite the derogatory words, had a low, velvety tone.

Dare tried to sit up but he was still too weak. Part of him did not want to be well. He worried that as soon as he was recovered enough, he'd be sent to the dungeon and he guessed that they did not have soft beds or pillows down there.

The man walked into the room a step and came into view, leaving the corridor shadows bereft.

He wore his velvets well. The waistcoat hugged his lean-ness, offsetting wide shoulders and narrow hips. His long sleeves puffed white as clouds. He wore no cloak or coat, but his buttons looked made of pure gold, as did the rings on both middle fingers. A wealthy courtier? Or a lord?

A tumble of tight, golden curls fell in wild twists to his shoulders. He wore no ornament in his hair. It looked as if it might be painful to run a comb through it, let alone entangle it with jewels.

"So you are the naughty prince rumors tell stories of."

"Rumors?" Dare asked.

The young man smiled, smooth tanned cheeks softening the hard angles of his cheekbones. "Stories spread by servants and chattel that roam from kingdom to kingdom with no country fealty."

"People who have supposedly met me?" Dare pushed his palms flat on the pillows at his sides and sat up. The room whirled, and then righted itself. His body felt light as air.

"They say," said the man, "that Prince Darius of Brookfall is somewhat anti-social. Schizoid. A bully. A demon."

Dare thought of how Darius, even when they were children, used to push the servant children and talk back to the adults and threaten them with beheading before he even knew what the word meant. As he got older, he made girls cry.

He punched Dare often. He punched servants. But he never actually formally punished anyone, even Dare. Being his footstool, and even his bed-warmer, Dare didn't really suffer. So the rumors were probably unfounded and he need not play up to them.

"I—I—" Dare started to speak.

"You look red in the face but I think that's the fever. Not demon characteristics."

"I don't know how rumors get started," Dare managed.

The man laughed, low and suspicious. "I don't know. You're from Brookfall and you're royalty. Proven to be at odds with us."

"Proven?"

"They say you were at the banquet when our delegation visited. One of the survivors—"

"Survivors?" Dare interrupted.

"Yes. Of the delegation."

"Some of them died?"

"You didn't know?" The man raised an eyebrow.

"No." Dare shook his head and it began to ache, confused by this elegant being in black velvet trousers and green velvet waistcoat trimmed in gold.

A guard's silhouette came around the edge of the healing room's doorway. "My lord, you should not be in here!"

The man turned his head with a quick jerk and said, "Do not presume to tell me what I should or should not do!"

"Apologies, my lord."

The guard's image vanished into the dark corridor beyond. Dare looked up, trying not to wince at his headache.

Now he knew the man speaking to him was a Lord. Who was he? He wanted to ask him. Instead, his mind kept imagining what could have happened to the Shastans who'd visited at court and so abruptly left after banquet held in their honor.

"How did they die?"

"The delegates were on their way home after your father threw them out into the night. They were beset upon by bandits in the Great Forest. Or maybe your father had them followed?"

"He wouldn't—"

"But against all rumors, there was one delegate who spoke highly of you. Used inane words like gracious, stylish, intelligent, kind. Swore you were the most well-mannered of hosts. Do you recall him?"

Dare thought of the man in the garden who'd called him handsome, and nodded. "I do." He blinked, closed his eyes for a moment. "I'm glad he survived."

"Are you?"

"Yes." Still, he wondered, could the king of Brookfall actually have been behind having the Shastan delegation ambushed?

"Why should I believe you?"

"I don't know why you should. I can only tell you that my father did not share many secrets with me."

"Yet you are eighteen. Of age to rule now. Wouldn't he be grooming you for the throne?"

Dare gulped. He'd known Darius to have many private meetings with his father. He had not been allowed to attend, but made to wait all those times alone and bored in the gray halls outside the king's chamber watching the daddy-long-legs make webs behind the oil lamp sconces.

"Yes," Dare finally said. "He was grooming me." He would have to make it up as he went, based on his lifelong observations of the real Prince Darius.

The lord frowned.

"But I didn't know members of your delegation had been killed," Dare said. "And I am truly sorry to hear of it."

"I want to believe you are lying. I want to believe you are the monster in the rumors. That we are enemies and you are a shit prince with no heart. I came to see for myself."

Finally, Dare got up the nerve to ask. "Who are you?"

"I want you to be hateful. Spiteful."

Dare sat very still, letting him vent. He was used it from royalty. Used to taking it, and compartmentalizing the insults into an area of his memory that he had created for such degradation, telling himself over and over that it was all part of the play, the roles and masks that royalty wore, and none of it was personal toward him.

The young lord went on. "I want you to be deserving of imprisonment so I can watch you held from freedom every day, and see you worry that maybe your father doesn't love you enough, that maybe he will do something that will allow us to punish you, to hurt you, to show your kingdom that we will be bullied no longer."

Am I deserving of punishment? Dare thought. If he were the true Prince Darius, this lord would be correct in his assumptions. Darius was not a good boy, nor at eighteen a good man. He was all the things this lord said he wished he was.

But Dare was not like that. And he was determined to play the role of the prince that should have been, deserving of a kingdom, a caring boy, a fair man who felt real empathy. Who was, in fact, born with a heart.

"Well," said Dare, and his voice came softer than he expected, tinged with his lingering illness, "you hardly know me. I'm currently in a sickbed. Admittedly, I'm not at my best."

When the man smiled, a new sort of look crossed his face than when he had chuckled at Dare's expense.

This time Dare saw something different in him, a soft beauty that he had failed to notice at first. And in the eyes, which were dark with shadows of their own, like Darius's but different somehow, edged with a sort of curiosity amid the suspicion, he saw a faint shine.

Darius's eyes had always had such an empty look. But this man's eyes were brimming with what Dare could only think of as a quickness of spirit. A yearning as if something waited within to be opened but was not yet revealed.

His breath caught at that smile.

The lord said, "You should be on your stomach and groveling. You should be begging for a dozen ways to prove yourself to me."

The words did not fit the smile that stayed on the stranger's face.

Who are you?

The man had never answered Dare's question. But Dare had his suspicions. For this man was the perfect age, and wore the perfect garb to be the prince of Shastan. Prince Malory. The Crown Prince. And the one the Shastan delegation, only weeks ago, had asked the King of Brookfall to give his son to. This was the man Prince Darius might have wed to keep the peace between their kingdoms. The man the

King of Brookfall had rejected, and thereby the entire kingdom as well.

He was sure of it now. Prince Malory stood before him, the victim of the highest of insults at this denied marriage proposal.

Dare said quietly, thoughts still racing, "I would prove myself to you. But I don't know how."

The prince gave a little smirk, but it wasn't as harsh as the looks Dare was used to receiving from Darius. "I don't know, either."

*

The next time he saw the man he thought of now as Prince Malory, Dare was sitting at a table by his bed, the first time he'd gotten out of bed in days. He was trying to finish a plate of toast. He felt cold, though the sun strode in on legs of bright silver through the high window. Dare wore a simple white nightshirt, unable to remember how he'd gotten it, and a thin, black cotton robe.

Apparently, he'd had some kind of infection of the body. No one really knew what it was but people got them often and sometimes they died and sometimes they didn't. He had been lucky that the Shastans had not denied him good medical care.

He had heard the guards in the outside hall during his convalescence and knew he was never left alone. People in Shastan feared him. Funny, since he was sick, unarmed, and only newly out of boyhood.

Now he heard a commotion as the door to his chamber opened, and a low but almost desperate guard's voice, "My lord, you should not be here—"

Surly. "Yes. I have been told this before."

"By orders of the king—"

"The king knows what he can do with his orders—"

Dare's eyebrows shot up. Shades of Darius? He still had nightmares of the prince dying in his arms every night. Darius had been a bully and brat, but had not deserved that death.

"Sire, it is only that—"

His words clipped. His voice commanding, compelling. "I shall be but a minute. No one needs to know!"

"But—"

Malory—for Dare had no more doubts the young man was the Shastan prince now—stepped through the threshold and slammed the heavy wooden door closed.

Dare brought his hands to his lap and looked up through his long tangles of bangs. He knew he probably looked a fright, unkempt and sick for so long.

The prince stood in the silvering light of early morning, a perfect specimen of the ruling class, not a wrinkle, not a jewel or button or buckle out of place. Except for his wild, weed-patch hair. Dare marveled at how golden it was, as if sprayed with gilt paint, though it must be only a trick of the light.

His black trousers tucked into knee-high boots, his billowing white shirt, his gold brocaded waistcoat, all stiff and new, expensive, set him apart with an air of commanding importance. A ruby set into an oval of dark metal sat on his chest against all that white cotton; it looked heavy and was affixed to a thick black chain.

Dare thought, *I should kneel. I should bow my head at least.*

But the prince had never asked it of him. Had yet to tell him on his own who he really was. Besides, he was still too sick to lever himself up on his own, so kneeling was out of the question.

We are both playing the imposter in this moment.

Dare stayed still and did not show obeisance.

Malory's eyes were dark, but a fire was in them so unlike Darius, who had shown nothing, ever, of any inner gleam.

Dare felt as if his fever might be returning as his face heated slightly at the thought.

Malory said, as if accusing him of something. "You're up."

"I am feeling better."

"You should. We have only the most excellent healers here."

"They have been very kind."

Malory tilted his head as if assessing him. He did not approach. He stood where he was, his back to the door, chin lifted.

He was very beautiful, like glimpsing a fae on a wooded hill in a dream.

Dare hesitated. "But I'm worried."

A stilted smile. "Why ever would you be?"

Dare's chest tightened. "What is to happen to me after I am well?"

"You're an enemy hostage."

"I know." Dare did not breathe for a moment.

"If your father maintains the peace, you will at least keep all your fingers and toes."

Dare gulped.

"You must know you deserve less."

Dare nodded once.

"You wonder where you will live, perhaps? The palace, of course. For you are royalty. But maybe the palace stables at first." He gave a short laugh. "Or the kitchens sweeping the ash away. Or maybe the dungeon. I heard the keeper tell the king just the other day he needed a new assistant. But the king will make the ultimate decision."

"I am lucky to be alive; I know this."

Malory watched him as if looking for some hidden agenda in his words.

"Did the guards who slaughtered your traveling troupe harm you?" He talked of it as if he were speaking of some harmless prank.

"No." Dare saw the blood again, everywhere on the billowing grasses, and the cook with his head missing. The guards sliced to pieces. And Darius dripping his life force onto his red velvet coat that Dare wore. He started to shake.

"You look pale," Malory said, and now he glanced away. "Maybe you should get back into bed."

Dare looked straight at him, trying to meet his eyes but the prince was now staring at the white-washed, brick wall.

"They didn't have to kill everyone. I was willing to go with them."

"That's not how the story got told."

"I offered myself. The guards wouldn't listen."

"Your own guard ignored your command?"

"It happened so fast. The confusion, the noise. They couldn't hear me; they were defending me, my—my honor."

"Of course that is why. I'm sure it wasn't incompetence. No, not at all." Malory turned away.

Dare felt as if his whole body was holding itself together by sheer will. He was shaking again, deep inside, and for some reason he did not want the prince to see.

Malory reached for the door handle, clicking it open with his thumb. He did not look over his shoulder as he left, but his voice came through clear and not without some threat. "I will speak to the healers. When you are well enough, you'll be brought to the king for his judgment on your fate."

The door snicked shut. The room seemed darker without the prince's presence. Charisma was what people called it when someone filled up a room with more than just their physical being. Not all rulers had it. Darius's showed up only in his innate ability to skillfully demean another one on one. But he had hated big gatherings, and meeting anyone new who wasn't a servant he could lord over.

This prince was different. Though unashamed at revealing his hatred for Dare, he showed a natural curiosity, if not more. It was enough to keep bringing him to Dare's healing chamber. Enough to blatantly disobey a king's command.

Dare stared at the closed door, halting in his breath.

It was too soon, he decided, to be out of bed this long.

He left his half-eaten breakfast and crawled back under the pillows and blankets, and slept.

Chapter Eight

The prince did not return.

The cloaked healers spoke little, asking questions more than answering them, but always gentle. In their healing practices, they did not see him as *other* but only a being in need.

Five days later, a healer appeared at the door, flanked by two guards.

Dare was up and dressed in well-worn black trousers that didn't quite fit (too big at the waist and had to be pinned), a stiff, beige muslin shirt with wooden toggles at the throat, and a blue vest that hung limp and did not fasten at the front.

He had asked about his other clothes, Darius's clothes, but was told by a healer they were too stained and could not be saved. He mourned that beautiful, red velvet coat.

They brought him the jewels he had worn—rings and a necklace—and he stuffed them in his pocket. He was happy to see the silver bracelet that had been his mother's was not lost. He put that on right away. The rest were far too fancy for his attire. They were worth a fortune, and he was surprised they allowed him to keep them.

The guards escorted him out of the room and into the dim hall. Soon, an open doorway led to the outside world and Dare had to blink hard in the daylight to adjust his aching eyes.

At first, he saw only the greenness, and the flitting of diaphanous insects through the grass. The courtyard sloped in a grassy expanse dotted with tiny, blooming star-flowers. As his eyes adjusted, a high wall of white brick came up in his view, wide enough to create a walkway on top, and guard towers every fifty paces or so. The towers jutted up into the sky, their pointed rooftops painted blue. Over the white balustrade and between the pillars that held the tower's second floor, he saw dark figures armed with bows.

The wall and its towers seemed to meander forever up the side of a hill, and Dare could see, finally, at the top, the Shastan palace.

The palace itself rose up hundreds of feet, a blue and purple spectacle of bannered turrets and balconies and round edifices and a hundred windows like eyes staring into the distance. Marbled steps led upward, nearly as wide as the palace itself. He could see the white columns framing the tall, large double doors, painted blue like the guard tower rooftops. Banners topped each side of those doors, emblazoned with a blue unicorn symbol.

He had not known this whole time if he had been inside the palace or not. But now he saw the healers' quarters were only miniscule outbuildings outside of the walled palatial estate.

The two guards pushed him onto a well-worn path that led up the hill.

As he neared the foregrounds, he saw a huge pond populated by at least a dozen gracefully-swimming, white swans. His heart beat fast to see them. In all the lands, swans were a symbol for greatness and change for the better. They glided here and there, making the dark blue waters shimmer with the trails they left behind. Willows lined the shore, their branches long and fluttering, dipping into the water's edge.

Flocks of white doves flew up and down the sides of the castle. He could hear them muttering and cooing along with the flapping of the banners in the high, slow breeze.

Servants moved up and down the trail before them, some with wooden carts, some with focused looks on their way to an errand or chore. They were all dressed somewhat as Dare was now, in lose clothing with unfastened, long vests of varying colors.

Dare had done what he could *not* to look like a mere servant. He'd washed well, including his hair, combing it back from his face. It hung long against his neck and shoulders, but at least it was neat. He'd seen himself in a hazy looking-glass when he shaved, and he was not too unfortunate-looking.

His legs shook a bit by the time he and the guards reached the top of the palace steps. Before they went in, the guards stopped him. One removed a set of manacles from his leather belt and put them on Dare's wrists, fastened in front.

Dare made no protest. As it was, no one had yet harmed him despite their past violence when abducting him.

Going from bright morning light into shadow again jarred him. But soon he saw dozens of sconces, all lit in the huge foyer, and high ceilings that reflected and refracted light from large windows to the right and left of the entrance.

The floor was rough-hewn marble tile the color of deep afternoon skies. The ceiling arched in one gigantic curve propped by no columns, only its own solid architecture which rivaled that of Brookfall.

Their footfalls echoed as they walked toward two more giant double doors as tall as two men. When they grew closer to them, Dare saw they were oak, and carved with intricate scenes of forest life complete with birds, foxes, wolves, and even the mythical unicorn, the Shastan royal crest.

Four guards wearing helms sprouting long black feathers guarded either side of the doors. When Dare and his guards approached, two moved toward the doors, opening them and letting the three of them pass through.

The throne room was full of people, servants standing at attention, courtiers dressed in their finest satins, velvets and silks, and guards along all sides gleaming in the finery of their breastplates, their helms, and with their polished broadswords at their sides.

The walls were solid white and carved with three-dimensional depictions of unicorns of all sizes and shapes prancing, rearing, bucking or grazing. So realistic. The carvings made the creatures look as if they might, at any moment, leap upon the throng lining the two sides of the court.

A line of dark blue carpet led to the throne itself, a raised dais upon which sat two thrones, one for the king, one for the queen.

Dare saw the king first. King Millard of Shastan had brown hair striped with gray tied back from his face. He wore a long gown of gold velvet belted with a heavy gold chain that sparkled with gems. The gown fell past his knees where he sat, revealing the leather of high boots. His cloak was emerald velvet lined with black satin. On his head sat a simple gold crown with one spike at the center, no jewel. He had a haggard face with a short graying beard and looked to be in his 40s.

A semi-circle of four guards stood motionless behind him.

The queen, whose name Dare still did not know, was small and round, about 40, and had a tumble of blonde hair that fell well past her sleeve-puffed shoulders. She wore a simple gown, all white with black trim. She had a severe, but pretty face. She stared at Dare with great interest.

But what interested Dare most was neither of them. Instead, his gaze sought the prince who stood between them, hands clasped behind his back, wearing colors that matched his father, a gold waistcoat over a green shirt, the usual black trousers that fit his slim form with snug perfection, and a lightweight cloak of pale gold satin that almost perfectly matched his twisting mat of hair.

Prince Malory's gaze locked onto Dare's eyes but no part of his face or body twitched. He never gave any indication they had met before.

Dare looked away as his guards led him forward.

The crowd in their gleaming, expensive fashions watched with glittering eyes. They'd all been waiting. Expecting him. Expecting Prince Darius.

He took a deep breath as he stopped in front of the throne before the three rulers. A guard bumped him with his elbow until Dare realized he was indicating that he should kneel.

He did so immediately, bowing his head and staring down at the plush, blue carpet. He focused on the way the fibers glinted in the light of dozens of oil lamps. The air was redolent with the sweet burn of them, as well as the perfumes of all the wealthy attendees, so many Dare could not guess the number. This day obviously promised to be a spectacle none of them wanted to miss.

"Prince Darius of Brookfall."

"Your Highness."

Dare wasn't sure if he should raise his head or not. In Brookfall, the king usually commanded the disciple before him to rise, no matter the ranking or occasion. But he was in a foreign country and the customs might be completely different. He needed to prove himself as a smart and kind ally, not the enemy they all still saw.

"You are a hostage of this empire and therefore relieved of all rights and privileges save those bestowed upon you by me, the queen, or my son, Prince Malory. Do you understand?"

"Yes, Your Highness," he said to the carpet.

"Then, you may rise, and answer questions as we put them to you."

Dare's heart skipped a beat as he pushed himself up to stand. He still felt weak from his fever, but well enough. His face burned. His vision glimmered. But he was used being put on the spot, treated like he had no rights anyway. He did not feel shy about it at all.

"First," said King Millard, "I wish to inform you that a message has been dispatched to your father and reportedly received. This message contained information to let him know we have you as a hostage, that no harm will come to you as long as all threats of war are tabled."

Dare kept his head bent, and did not respond.

"Are you aware that your father's army still stands at the ready on the border by Chikatek?"

"No, Your Highness."

"Ten thousand men. He was ordered to stand down. He has made no other threatening moves but his men remain at the border."

Dare's heart rate sped up.

"Are you and the king close, Prince Darius?"

"Close, Your Highness?"

"I am asking if your father even cares if you live or die."

"Yes, Your Highness." But he wasn't entirely sure. He knew Darius thought his father a fool. And the king knew Darius to be spoiled and a coward who did not like public functions, let alone travel.

"Then if I send another rider to Chikatek with a demand to stand down or you will be punished, will he agree?"

Dare let out a short breath. "I hope so, Your Highness."

"This we shall all hope for, of course, the best outcome for us all. In the meantime, the question put to me is where to house you until we receive word from the king of Brookfall."

"Is he well enough for the stockades?" the queen asked, brow narrowed in distrust. "He should be sent there anyway. A ward of the dungeon-master."

If Dare thought the queen's looks were severe, he realized her voice was worse. Pitched to a minor melodic tone, it cut like a blade.

"Prince Darius, do you wish harm upon our country?" Prince Malory spoke for the first time. Dare wanted to look at him but remained still.

"No, Your Highness. Never."

"Were you aware that your father the King of Brookfall wished to make a first strike against us?" Malory asked.

"Yes, Your Highness. But not why." It was the truth. The insult at the banquet the king had felt when the Shastans had made the offer of marriage between their countries had been the final push that sent the king into a rage. But there had to have been more reason for him to want to declare war.

Dare wove his fingers together, feeling the coolness of the manacles against his upper hands.

"Where were you headed when your party was caught by our guard?" asked Malory.

"To the Summer Chateau. It's on the Ryn Gorge east of the Great Forest."

"You were not to join your father's army, why?"

Dare shifted once on his feet. "He wanted me out of the way, Your Highness."

"So you're not a warrior."

Dare heard a soft footfall and looked upward without moving his head to see the prince had descended the dais by one step. His black leather boots shone with glints of silver and blue light.

"I am no warrior, Your Highness," Dare replied in almost a whisper.

"We would like to know what your father's plans entailed," Malory said.

"My father did not share his detailed plans with me," Dare replied, hoping they believed him. If Darius knew, that knowledge had died with him. "He confided only with his inner court circle, Your Highness."

"Why would he not confide in his only heir, the Crown Prince of Brookfall?"

"I—I—" Dare stumbled on his own tongue.

"Is something wrong with you that your own father left you outside important decisions of the realm?"

The prince was taking over this question and answer session, it seemed, and it was as if he and Dare had never met.

"Are you daft in the head?" the prince asked.

"No, Your Highness. At least, I don't think so."

The court erupted in a wave of laughter. People in the room shifted, jewels chiming, stiff satins and raw silks rustling. Leather rubbing against itself in soft rasps and squeaks.

"Then there must be some reasoning behind your father's actions to exclude you. Or you are a liar."

Dare saw an opening and took it. Who would know any better if he lied or not? He could compose any story of his life and it would be the same. Their belief in him was out of his control.

"In truth, Your Highness, I did not wish to say it in public and be deemed a traitor. But my father and I did not get along well at all." He could tell his own truth, for the king of Brookfall had mostly ignored him his whole life unless he did something praiseworthy of a servant.

"Your reputation precedes you," the prince said. "You are known as lazy, insolent, spoiled and stupid by my people. But I confess we are quick to accept such rumors from a country that has mostly despised us."

"If I may speak, Your Highness?"

Dare turned his head to see who had spoken.

A man stepped forward and out the corner of his eye Dare saw it was the same young delegate who'd walked with him in the perfumed night of the Brookfall castle gardens. The man who'd touched him gently, laughed with him, called him lovely.

"You may, Chancellor Brig," the king replied.

"I only met Prince Darius once. When I visited Brookfall, Prince Darius was the most gracious of all the hosts, polite and flawless in his demeanor with the public. I found him outgoing, friendly, in fact. He showed no animosity toward our people and seemed shocked and confused when the king threw us out of his hall."

The king seemed to grumble before he said, aloud, "Does anyone else here have words to say about Prince Darius?"

70

Another delegate Dare did not remember stepped forward. "I can confirm Chancellor Brig's testimony, Your Highness. Though I never actually spoke to the boy one on one, he was a gracious host."

"Thank you for your testimony, Chancellors."

The two men bowed and backed away to the crowd.

"My purpose here," said King Millard, "is to decide where Prince Darius should reside and how he shall be treated. He is of royal blood, not a servant, and yet the crimes of his country against ours cannot be denied. An enemy hostage should be chained and under guard at all times. But our promise to not harm him unless his father upsets the peace must also be kept."

Through his eyelashes, Dare saw the king look to the queen.

"I say the stockades are good enough for him. Then the dungeon. Where all prisoners of war are kept," she said.

"Since there is no war," Prince Malory offered, "he is not a prisoner of war. As a hostage of royal blood, he should have a warm room here in the palace. Under guard at all times, of course."

"Thank you both for your input." The king stood. He was tall and lean like his son. His cloak billowed gently about him, rippling to the floor in emerald cascades.

"Prince Darius." The king's voice echoed through the huge room. "I command you to look at me now."

Dare raised his chin. His eyes met the king's gaze which was not friendly but not hateful, either.

"You are an enemy hostage of this court. Do you understand?"

Dare nodded. "Yes, Your Highness."

"You are not free to come and go. Yet I hesitate in giving you over to the dungeon-master, for we have no evidence of any crimes you have committed against us. You have recently been very ill, and a relapse might mean your death, and then we will have no bargaining power. I am in agreement with my son that you should be given rooms befitting your class here in the palace."

The queen made small gasp of disgust.

"However, you will be fitted with a collar and chain. You will go nowhere unaccompanied by your guards. At public meals, should I deign to allow you to attend them, and on that matter I have not yet decided, you will be chained to your chair. When walking about, only the guards will have control over your chain. Orders to the contrary will be ignored unless coming from myself, my queen, or my son. You will remain unharmed unless your father does not abide by the contract we've sent him. Do you understand your two roles here? That you are to obey your guards' every command. And that you are a hostage until negotiations end."

"Yes, Your Highness."

The guards on either side of him gripped him under the arms and pulled him around and toward the back of the room. Fear clutched him for a split-second, and he stumbled.

"Get up," said the one on his left.

He hadn't quite fallen, he'd just tripped over his own feet. The impatient guard grumbled under his breath.

This was the moment he made the final commitment. To be Prince Darius. There was no turning back. No time to think. If they found out he was a servant now, a servant the real Prince Darius had nicknamed Footstool, surely his life would be over.

For a moment, his vision went white. His stomach felt funny. *Just don't let me throw up on this pretty blue carpet.*

When they reached the double doors, they opened, guards standing to either side of the entrance. Dare's guards pushed him forward and out into the grand foyer.

When they headed for the outside doors, Dare said, "Where are we going?"

He had thought he was to be given a palace room.

"First things first," said the guard on his right. "You have to be fitted for the collar."

Chapter Nine

"The king did not specify the metal."

"You cannot have a prince in irons!"

"You can if he's a traitor prince!" Laughter.

The conversation went on over Dare's head as if he wasn't there.

"He is the guest of the king. He'll be living in the palace."

"He's a hostage. In chains."

"The palace has a reputation to uphold for fashion, for elegance, for expensiveness."

"For intelligence?"

More laughter.

"For diplomacy and fairness. Your drunk-talk borders on offense to the Crown."

"Bask, you killjoy. You take everything so seriously. Lighten up."

The two guards and the blacksmith kept chattering. Finally, the blacksmith said, "Gold. The king will expect no less. I'll take the measurements and it will be done by tomorrow. In the meantime, I have this ugly thing as a temporary collar."

It was indeed iron. Black and worn thin at the edges. It looked sharp.

"Maybe you can keep him out of the king's sight for a day?"

The blacksmith said to Dare, "Tilt your chin up, head back."

Dare obeyed. The blacksmith pressed the collar to this throat. "Hold back your hair," he said.

Dare's hands were manacled. He didn't move.

Bask said, "Damn it." He reached out and gathered Dare's hair to one side in his fist, tugging.

Dare winced.

The blacksmith fiddled for a few seconds, and then said, "It needs a little adjustment."

When the collar locked into place, the heaviness of it threatened to choke Dare. He shrugged his shoulders, trying to get it to settle further down. But every time he swallowed, his Adam's apple pressed tight against the inside.

He coughed.

"It's too tight," Dare said.

Bask said, "It's not meant for your comfort."

Dare's eyes blurred.

"Is it choking you?" the blacksmith asked.

"I can't swallow properly."

Bask slid two fingers inside the collar, his fingernail scratching Dare as he did it. "It's fine. He's not choking."

"It's sitting wrong. It's right against my throat."

The other guard crossed his arms over his chest and assessed the situation. He was older, with creases about his dark eyes. "The collar is for bondage, not torture. It's not coming off him without the key, so loosen it a thumbnail's width."

The blacksmith did as told and the collar, while still heavy and tight, didn't press his throat as much.

Dare said nothing as he stood up, but the discomfort remained. He wondered if he'd ever get used to it.

*

The first thing Dare saw when the guards ushered him into his new room was a long window, square at the bottom, curved at the top. At either side were gathered curtains, royal blue with a scattered printing of white stars. At its base was a cushioned seat just like the one he favored back home.

74

Chained, a prisoner, he would still be able to sit and look out, watch the pathways beyond the castle walls, the grasses blowing in the wind, and the magnificent swans on their miniature sapphire lake.

But there was more.

Far from being a dank, damp cell, next his eye was drawn to the massive bed covered with purple and blue quilts, and canopied. The drapes that drew to the sides with black metal chains were the same blue as the curtains on the window.

Two, unlit six foot tall, iron candelabras were in place—one beside the foot of the bed, one at the head, both well away from the drapes. A wooden table with two smaller candelabras and a high-backed chair fit snugly on the other side of the window. A wardrobe against one wall, doors open, showed a line of white shirts, black trousers, and fancy waistcoats much nicer than what he now wore. A pair of polished black boots sat in front of the wardrobe.

This was to be his residence?

Bask shoved him forward. "Your room. Fit for an enemy prince, I suppose. You're lucky you're of royal blood. Hostages never get quarters as fine as these."

Dare easily kept his footing after the shove. He'd been pushed so often by Darius he'd learned supreme balance. He rarely fell.

Ignoring his guards now, he looked up, mouth dropping open. The ceilings stretched higher than two tall men standing one on the other's shoulders. Where the smooth, white wall met the edge were deep carvings of beautiful, flowing humans with long, naked torsos, their legs disappearing into the wall, bent trees with their branches flowing along the ceiling-line, and unicorns and stags, some with just their heads poking out as if through the structure itself. Everything smelled fresh, like the fragrance of rain having just passed through.

The floor of wood planks was not rough but smooth, as if you could run with bare feet across it and never get splinters. The only rug was an oval of rough-woven wool, black and soft, by the side of the bed.

A loud bang sounded behind him.

Dare whirled to face the closed door. He heard a lock snick shut.

He was alone, now, and all his muscles seemed to turn liquid at once. He moved to the chair, leaned against it, and took a deep breath.

For as long as he had to, he could live here. Yes. His own room. No dungeon or dungeon-master. His only worry that the King of Brookfall might be insane enough to sacrifice his only son and heir to a selfish act of war.

He couldn't think about that right now. After the stress of the morning, he was thirsty.

On the table he found a pitcher of cool water, and a wooden cup. He drank, then poured himself more and took the cup to the window seat.

The collar pulled at his neck, scratching. The loose, thick chain dangled all the way to the floor, making a scraping sound as he walked.

But as he sat and looked out, reveling in the countryside view, he counted himself lucky. For the time being, he was alive, his fever had been cured, and the Shastans did not seem unduly cruel despite the queen's animosity and desire to see him in the stockade.

And the prince. Malory. Was he on Dare's side or not? Thinking of him, the tall man with the untamed hair, Dare's stomach fluttered. Malory had been the one to suggest housing him in the palace. Was it compassion, or did he simply want to keep an eye on the enemy?

Dare hoped for the first. Malory had clearly been disobeying the king's orders when he had twice visited Dare. The first time, curiosity had been the obvious reason. A confrontation of sorts. But the second time had been something more. But curiosity still existed, and maybe a hint of concern.

He sipped at the water and winced into the bright day through the window. The light stung him but it also warmed him. He watched through watery eyes as two white swans glided across liquid blue. Pure and serene.

He tried to relax but everything was still so new. And past images continued to rear. Blood and death. Darius in his arms so hollow and empty. Cruel toward life even in the end, eyes wide with pain and hate for a world that offered him nothing, but retaining enough faculty to give the order to Dare. *Be me.*

It was Darius's last cruelty, for he had given prince-hood to Dare, which he despised and which had offered him nothing but an ability to get away with being bad and unhappy. Given it to him not as a gift, but as a curse. A burden. For he knew punishment awaited him at the hands of the Shastans. And he wanted Dare to take it. To suffer.

No truer or more horrible person had he known than Darius. It was as if his parting words were, "If I have suffered, so must you. That's my last order to you, Footstool."

*

Several hours later, the door to Dare's new room opened and a servant brought in a tray of food, placing it on the table by the high-backed chair. Out in the corridor, Dare saw the shadows of guards and sensed their irritation at their lowly job of guarding the enemy.

"Thank you," he said to the servant, a kitchen-girl not more than fourteen.

She bowed her head. "It is the leftovers from the royal lunch."

Dare saw fresh rolls, two apples, three pieces of chicken, and a pot of hot tea. On a smaller plate sat a square of cake, iced white.

"It all looks good."

She merely nodded, hesitant as if unsure what to do. He knew the thought had crossed her mind to curtsey. But she had seen the collar and chain. He was not her lord, nor her better.

After he ate as much of the lunch as he could manage, he found a stack of books on a shelf in the wardrobe and sat in the window's light on the cushion and read a book of fairytale stories.

He fell asleep against the sill and woke coughing, having dreamt Darius's hands were around his neck, pressing tight. He clawed at the black, metal collar, shifting his body to find a better position.

He heard a noise by the door and turned his head.

"You'll get used to it."

Malory stood in the doorway. A guard stood behind him, sneering, pissed.

"What?" Dare asked, trying to compose himself.

"The collar. After awhile, it will feel normal, almost as if it's not there."

Dare watched the way he moved into the room, shutting the door behind him right in the guard's face. He walked as if he weighed nothing. An effortless and quiet stride. He peered over Dare's shoulder to the courtyard.

Dare felt the sudden warmth of him, too close, and something else. As if the air, affected by the prince, singed his cheeks and the backs of his hands. Something in his stomach turned over.

"Ah, nice view. Lucky."

Malory had come to talk?

"I used to consider myself lucky," Dare said. "To have all I needed. To live in a castle."

"Lucky to be born royal?" Malory asked, confused.

Dare balked for a moment. He had been thinking of how he'd served Darius, and without that job he'd have been nothing, an orphan, a waif.

"Yes," he finally answered. "Lucky to be born a prince."

"After this morning, now you know who I am."

"I already knew who you were, Prince Malory. From your first visit in the healing compound."

"I suppose it takes a prince to know a prince."

"I suppose." Dare hesitated to say more. If a prince could recognize his own kind, maybe Malory would start to see truth. But no, Dare had been raised with a prince his whole life, and he knew how to play the role even better than Darius did.

"Then you know we were to be matched," Malory continued, taking no notice of Dare's nervousness.

Dare's muscles clenched, a strange burn simmering in his veins. Softly, "Yes."

"What did you think of that, when the Shastan delegation made the proposal? Your father went quite mad, I hear. But you?"

"I didn't know until later." He thought of Darius laughing derisively, telling him of the ridiculous offer.

"That is not an answer."

"I—I would have obeyed my father's command."

"You didn't hate the idea?"

Dare lifted his eyebrows in surprise. "No."

Darius had hated it. He would have been a poor match for Malory. Dare tried to imagine the two of them together. Had the Shastan proposal been accepted, Darius would have bargained for a fake marriage and probably dallied servant girls, or boys, on the side. And played with his own private servant, Footstool, if he'd had a thought to bringing Dare with him. He would never have allowed Malory into his aloof and private life. His spoiled laziness. He would have hidden himself away, claiming the Shastans were boring and the world an ugly place, not good enough for the likes of him.

"Why would I hate the idea?" Dare ventured.

"We'd have had to adopt heirs. And put up with the criticism of those who hate royalty for its quirks, doing things wrong or strangely, against fashion, against nature," Malory said.

"But we would be following a king's order. Unquestioned and above reproach from any public criticism. No one would dare—" Dare stopped.

Malory looked at him through tight eyes, and lowered lashes. His eyebrows nearly met.

Dare caught his breath. Maybe Malory hadn't wanted it in the same way Darius hadn't. A forced contract. Promises to a stranger. But Malory, though he presented an air of getting everything he wanted, and of some conceit, did not seem like Darius at all. He was wary of a stranger in their midst, but had not been mean. He'd spoken up for Dare when he'd stood in front of the king.

"You're saying you would have accepted the contract?" Malory turned away, as if speaking on a subject casual to him.

"I would have been willing."

"Your reputation does not match your words."

"You said it yourself. Rumors, only. You are here in front of me, speaking to me. You can decide my reputation for yourself."

Malory turned back to face him, the light from the window flashing against his dark eyes. "I decide everything for myself. No one tells me what to do."

"Like visiting me when your father forbids it?"

He let out a hard breath. A hiss. "You don't know a thing about me."

Dare lifted his chin. He'd known princes his whole life. He would play this well, for his very life. "Nor do you about me."

The way Malory turned in, pretending to examine the room and ignore him, told Dare much. The prince wanted to know. His stance, his very being, exuded interest. And Dare

80

knew then that Malory had been curious about more than an enemy prince.

Dare wondered what it might have been like, the two of them, married and honoring that contract. Malory had wanted to see him so he could imagine it. Maybe even fantasize about it. Now he could see it in him. Malory was less like Darius, more like Dare. Curious. Not hateful. And he liked boys. Perhaps he'd wanted this.

But now the proposal had been withdrawn. Now there was no chance—

Dare watched as Malory scratched at his unruly hair, moving from foot to foot. He was silent too long, and he kept wincing a little with each breath. Finally, he went to the bed and sat hard on the edge, bouncing, stomping his feet against the dark rug there.

"What are you like, then?" he asked, still not looking at him. "Other than the monster you were rumored to be throughout the two realms."

Dare felt his mouth curve up, and a softness behind his eyes. He liked the inquisitiveness of the prince. He was "Footstool". He played the part of the prince when Darius wanted him to. Now he was playing another part. Himself, but also a prince. Lying and telling the truth. The best he could do was go slowly.

"I supposed I am still trying to find myself. Who I am, what—"

"You don't have to over-think your answer," Malory interrupted. "But—well—you were being taken faraway from potential war. Are you a coward?" His boots tapped at the rug as if he could not keep still.

"My father wanted me protected as his only heir."

"Can you fight?"

"Yes. A very small amount with the broadsword. And the edgeless. I'm better with the small-sword."

"Who isn't?"

He remembered practicing with Darius, letting him win every time in each category. He was stronger but never let it show. And Darius got bored with the lessons so easily. Their training had been imperfect.

"How old are you?"

"Nineteen next month. And you?"

Malory glanced aside. "Twenty-three." His knees still went up and down, an interesting quirk of nerves. Though he affected such a look of unconcern.

Dare nodded. Twenty-three and unmarried. It was rare for royalty. He did not comment.

"What else do you want to know?"

"Oh, the usual three 'f's." Malory leaned to the side on one elbow, stopped the movement of his bouncing knees as if noticing it now.

"Three 'f's?"

"First kill. First fuck. Favorite color."

Dare's smile widened. "Why would you be interested at all? I'm the enemy."

"Haven't you heard the quote?"

"What quote?"

"Keep your friends close, your enemies closer."

"If there is a war, you think I can provide you with inside information?"

"Maybe."

"I'm no traitor."

Malory raised a dark gold eyebrow. "Good. Because the only thing I despise worse than a traitor is a royal from Brookfall."

Dare watched the light angle itself on the floor with bent, white edges. So Malory despised him. That meant this was an interrogation. Not friendly curiosity.

What would Darius have done? Probably laughed in his face. Or spat. Or even gotten up, walked over to the bed and punched him. Not caring that it might mean a change of venue from palace to dungeon.

Dare could do none of those things because they weren't in his nature. He said, "If you are predisposed to despise me then why do you care to ask me any questions at all?" He longed to tug at his collar but kept his hands still.

"You never know when information of any kind might prove valuable."

He reminded himself this man had come to visit him twice while Dare was sick. Malory had been the one to suggest his accommodations not include a straw bed and a damp, stone floor in a lightless room.

"That goes both ways," said Dare.

Malory gave him a half-smirk. "My father does not want me talking to you. He thinks you're a threat."

Dare had never thought of himself as dangerous. Not for one moment. How quickly things changed. Footstools could become liars and princes overnight.

"Well, I don't think of myself as a threat."

"You should. How do you expect to rule without inspiring some amount of fear in not only your subjects, but your advisors? Respect is earned through strength."

"Strength can also be shown in compassion. In listening. And in giving respect in return," Dare said.

"You're soft. Opposite from your reputation."

"I'm not soft." Dare heard the defensiveness in his tone only after the words were out. He backed up, started again. "My father is a tyrant. I don't see the point in ruling just like him. It's unnecessary."

"You do not admire him?"

Dare wondered if he should answer true. Neither he nor Darius had ever liked the man behind the king. "Not as much as he would wish it."

"Sooo, you and your father don't get along."

"I didn't say that."

He thought back on all the meetings Darius had had with the king while Dare waited in the empty, dim hall. How Darius had come out of those meetings in foul tempers, ready to make Dare's life a little harder. Kicking, pushing, blaming him for everything. Once, Darius had said, "You take my place at public functions. I wish you could also take my place in my father's chambers. He's such a self-centered bastard he might not even notice."

Malory said, "You didn't have to say it. It's evident on your face."

Dare looked up from the light patterns on the floor.

Malory watched him with a narrowed gaze. Edgy. Flashing with some inner burn. Or need.

"He is not a warm man. But he is my father," Dare said.

"Mine likes to make a lot of rules with set punishments if they're broken." Malory's smile was shrewd. "But he's not a bad man."

Dare decided to be honest. "I am sorry if my father insulted your people. I was given information that told me he himself felt insulted. But that is never a reason--"

"Are you? Sorry?" he interrupted.

"Yes. And I'd like to add I'm not your enemy. I'm not anyone's enemy in Shastan. And I don't consider you one."

"Why not? Our guardsmen killed all the people in your traveling party."

"It was because they wanted me and my people wouldn't give me up."

"See? We wanted the prince for a hostage. Now you are here. We're enemies."

Dare closed his eyes tight. Remembering. "The worst part was that I was willing to go with your guards. To avoid the violence. But no one would listen."

When he opened his eyes, Malory was staring at him as if he'd just seen him for the first time.

Dare's eyes stung. "If I could've made one person hear me, it might have been a different outcome."

"Well," Malory said off-hand. "Men are trained to fight." The words seemed harsh but the prince's tone had lowered. "The world's a rough place."

"That's what Darius—" He stopped himself. Shocked that for a moment he'd forgotten who he was supposed to be.

"What?"

"My personal servant shared my same name. Darius. He used to say the world was ugly. That you could trust no one."

"And now here you are telling me this and you don't even know me."

"I have to start somewhere. I don't know anyone in this country. Other than the healers, you're the only one who's come to talk to me. Or asked me any questions other than what the king asked me this morning."

"Yes. I know. And I should be off. I have better things to do." Malory jumped up from the side of the bed, striding to the door.

Dare blinked, eyes still aching. To be dismissed by the one person who had seemed to show an interest in him felt worse than when Darius had used him as a footstool. At least then he had Darius's attention. And he knew what was expected of him.

Here in Shastan he was alone and no one cared. And the King of Brookfall was just crazy enough that it was possible he might forego the safety of his only son.

Then Dare would be well and truly doomed.

The door to his chamber slammed shut. Instead of turning to look outside, he stared at the back of that door for a long, long time.

Chapter Ten

The pond lapped at its brown banks. The swans bent along the water's surface, gliding in silent grace. The serenity could not be denied, but Dare saw only an unattainable world. Everything had always been beyond his reach. Now, as a prisoner—a hostage—he had been drawn even further away from life.

The guards walked a little behind him, one on either side, as they made their way along the path from the blacksmith's workshop near the palace barn. The guard to Dare's left held his chain as if he were a pet. No, less than a pet. A pet would have the affection of its owner, and a reason for being. Dare had none.

His new collar was smooth and warm against his neck. Much lighter. It did not hurt him like the rough iron one had, but it still constricted him. It pressed the side of his neck in such a way that he could feel every tremor of his heartbeat. As if that, too, was chained, the very pulse that gave him life.

Hoof beats sounded on the soft grass behind them.

Dare turned his head. A group of riders trotted past, coming from the barn. At the head of the party strode a man with gold-bramble hair, and he rode tall, back straight, in perfect form.

As the group passed, Malory turned his head and met Dare's eyes, looking him up and down. In the outside daylight, Malory's eyes looked almost amber. Hyper-aware. His gaze took Dare in and Dare's entire body lightened, as if he were being lifted up by that look.

In another life, another world, Dare might be one of that group riding alongside the prince and feeling the wind on his face.

Malory was turned almost all the way around in his saddle now. Only when he was some distance away, did he turn and not look back. They headed for the castle gate.

"Where are they going?" Dare asked Hoop.

"A hunting party. They're going to the fire gorge for the day."

"Who are the men with the prince?"

"Courtiers' sons. Boys he grew up with. Lords in their own right as well."

He would never be one of them. He had accepted that even all the times he played the part of the prince. He took a deep breath to ease the ache in his chest.

*

Dare watched out his window for the return of the hunting party. He didn't want to be watching, but he couldn't help himself.

The sky turned pink. The swans swam into the willows' shadows. Servants shouted to each other along the path, laughing. He heard, distantly, someone practicing the flute. The casement window was opened partway, letting in the soft air of pre-evening. For a moment he felt lost in a long forgotten tale from a book. A tale of a prince locked in a tower waiting for someone to come with the key. Waiting for the world to change.

Beyond the palace he saw black mountains with white peaks. In the foreground, what wasn't hidden by the stone walls, he saw a sloping meadow carpeted with orange flowers. Poppies. Even in the courtyard, the poppies had started to appear everywhere, overtaking the starflowers, proclaiming spring. It seemed as if they had bloomed overnight. They smelled of tangy sweetness.

When he had gone to the blacksmith's that morning, he'd bent and picked some, crushing them into his small vest pocket. Now those flower petals decorated his sill, bent but still whole. Giving off their special fragrance.

It would be full night soon. The hunting party was late.

When Dare finally saw them arrive, the sky had turned a limitless dark blue with creases of deep pink in the west where the hills rolled low off the mountainsides. They were all there, six horses, six riders, but he heard a shout from one of the towers near the gate where three bronze torches burned.

From the front of the palace, servants came running. One of the riders headed toward them while the rest turned for the stables. The servants helped the rider off his horse, surrounding him as they moved to the palace entrance, and then Dare lost sight of them.

But he had seen, even in the dimness, that cloud of blond hair reflecting the early starlight.

*

Dare stared at the words in his book but didn't see them. At this point in the evening, Darius would have been whining for him to finish his homework for him. Invariably, it would be geography or history, both of which the Brookfall prince had deemed "mortally boring".

Now all he could think about was what might have happened on that hunt. Why had Prince Malory arrived as if he needed help?

Dare imagined all manners of injuries and wasn't sure why it obsessed him so. Malory had been alive. He had not been carted into the palace, though he had been supported by the strongest male servants. Whatever had happened to him was most likely minor.

When the young servant girl delivered his dinner he asked her if she knew what had happened.

She shook her head. So shy. "No, m'lord."

He followed her to the door and asked the guards. Bask and a guard named Derek were on duty.

Bask shoved him back inside without answering and closed the chamber door in his face.

After eating, Dare paced his room, dragging his chain along the floor. This chain was different from the first chain he had worn, a more delicate chain of fine steel links attached to the new, pure gold collar he'd been fitted with today.

He had the errant thought that between this gold collar and the jewels of Darius's he'd been wearing when he'd been taken, and which they'd let him keep, if he ever escaped he'd have plenty of money to start a new life. He had no clue what he might do on his own. He did know he would not want to return to Brookfall. They thought him dead anyway.

But at the moment, plans of escape did not occupy his mind. He had a role to play more important than his own needs. Maintaining his perfect mask meant reprieve from war for two large realms.

Back and forth he paced, from window to door. Malory's face kept pushing into his mind. And in the background, he saw Darius's smirk and heard his smile-less laughter.

He was used to Darius and could ignore him even if his subconscious mind could not. But Malory he could not disregard. Every time he thought of him his stomach gave a little flip, his heart a hesitant but hopeful leap.

It was stupid of him, he knew. Malory had called him enemy. Malory hated him. Yet he'd also said he wanted to know about him. *First fight. First fuck. Favorite color.*

They had never talked of any of those things. Malory had obviously put those questions into the air as hypothetical when what he was really after was useful information on the weaknesses of Brookfall and its king. Dare reminded himself Malory had shown interest for political reasons. But deep inside he could not quell the feeling that Malory's visits meant something more.

Dare put his hands on the sides of his head and tugged at his hair. His feelings—his hope—that Malory might befriend him needed to cease.

Yet he could not stop thinking about how Malory had ridden up to the palace steps, come off his horse into the arms of servants and disappeared.

He could feel the pulse in his throat hammering against the gold collar.

This would not do at all.

*

Dare had slept fitfully and risen bleary-eyed, having eaten only half his breakfast.

The chamber door opened and Bask appeared in the entryway.

Dare looked up through his dark, tangled bangs. Maybe the guards wanted to go for a walk.

"You are requested."

"What?"

Bask shrugged. "You are to follow me."

"I'm only half-dressed."

"Then get dressed."

Dare threw off his dressing gown and quickly put on trousers and a shirt, feeding the chain through the neck so it would hang outside the cloth and down the center of his body in front. It was useless, really. They never used it the chain except to lead him around. The steel burned cold against his skin. Now it was cushioned and he could barely feel it at all.

He quickly pulled on his boots, ran his fingers through the worst of his hair-snarls, and approached the door with chain in tow to hand it to the guard. Bask took the chain and led him like a dog on a leash. The second guard followed behind him.

The corridor had plain gray walls interspersed with sconces to light the way. They quickly reached a stairwell and

Dare expected them to go up, but Bask tugged his chain and led him down through shadows of stairs and into kitchen smells of roasting meats, fresh baked breads and the hot scent of ovens and woodstoves. Soon he could hear the banging of kitchen sounds, and servant voices echoing.

Just before they reached the kitchens, Bask stopped and turned to face the wall. Three holes Dare might never have noticed dented the wall. Bask put his fingers into them and pulled and a piece of the wall from the floor to about five feet up broke away neatly, making a soft scraping sound as it opened. Beyond that was another door made of wood. Bask took a key and opened it and they all ducked as they went through.

Inside stretched a hidden hall drenched in darkness. Bask dropped Dare's chain and took two torches off an inside wall and lit them from a lantern the other guard carried.

Dare held his own chain now as they moved forward within the orb of light the torches made for them. They hadn't moved more than ten steps before he nearly gasped. Revealed before him were walls painted with colorful frescos. First, the images were birds. Singles. Then flocks.

As they walked, the walls revealed the skies of the birds in flight puffed with clouds. Suns and stars followed. All colors, bright as if they had been painted yesterday, had been used to make this grand mural. The skies gave way to detailed forests thick with trees, animals, flowers, mushrooms.

Then came the people, life-sized, some in royal garb, some in peasant clothes. Their faces were all unique, some looked happy or sad, others weather-beaten, old. Some were children with colorful toys: balls, dolls, toy horses, toy carts. Moving along, landscapes changed from meadows to mountains.

The secret hall had an arched, low ceiling and the walls curved upward, the frescoes continuing overhead as well with flowing vines, jungles of flowers, garden gates, little ponds.

"Who did all this?"

Bask said, "No one knows how it got started. But local artists come once in awhile to freshen it up, keep it nice."

"But it's hidden. No one sees it."

"Some do. Those who have the keys to the secret passageways."

They turned up a narrow staircase, then turned again to climb another. The torchlight revealed more stunning murals of unicorns, men and women with wings, giant dragons puffing bouquets of flowers.

When they got about three levels up, Bask produced his key again and opened a door to another passage that led from narrow shadow straight into the regular, gray corridor. They stopped in front of a great oak door.

Bask said, "You are not to speak of this visit, as it is unsanctioned at this time."

Unsanctioned by the king, Dare thought.

Now he knew where he was.

Bask knocked. A servant boy opened the door, then stood back and said, "Just the prince."

Bask gave Dare a little shove. Dare, still holding his own chain, stepped into the flickering light from within and into a huge room decorated in red and purple velvets, the floor lined with hand-woven rugs to match. There were three windows on two walls. This was a corner room and he could see that double doors, the top halves made of glass, opened to a vast balcony.

The room held too many things to look at all at once. Furniture, tapestries, artwork, sculptures, high-backed chairs, benches, shelves with rocks, crystals, books and games. But the central focus of the suite was the bed. It looked made of gold, both head and footboards, and the feet. Its posts supported a canopy at least nine feet in height and was draped in dozens and dozens of sheer, thin silks all black and lavender and dark blue like the colors of a storm.

The color palette of the room was dark, which made the room dim despite all the windows. But still Dare could see on that wide, big bed a reclining figure in a black satin dressing gown, one bandaged foot raised on a brocaded pillow with gold fringe, his blond head and broad shoulders leaning on about three more fancy bolsters. He had a book in one hand, a chalice in the other. He looked up.

Dare heard the door close behind him.

Chapter Eleven

"Prince Darius. You are here. Good. I was so bored."

Without thinking, he said, "Call me Dare."

"All right. Dare." Malory squinted. "Come closer. The way the light is in here you're all silhouette."

Slowly, Dare moved forward, heart beating hard again in his throat, the rush of it pressing his collar. He wasn't sure what to think, or why he was here.

Another spoiled prince. Another spoiled prince's room. He would not allow himself to wish it would be any different than with Darius. It didn't matter that the Shastans, and Malory himself, thought him a prince. He was a stranger. A hostage. The enemy.

"What am I doing here?" he asked.

"The other men my age are always trying to court my favor no matter what. They compete with each other. It's tedious. You, well, you have nothing to prove. I wanted to play some cards, or backgammon with someone who might not let me win for a change."

Dare walked closer to the bed, looking at Malory's foot. "How did you get hurt?"

"Stupid, really. We were going too fast chasing a stag. Another horse bumped mine in the side. Really hard. Right into my leg. The ankle's broken a bit, not bad, and the healers say it will be fine. I'm to stay off it for six weeks. I think I'll go mad before then."

Dare responded with a tentative smile. "I'd be happy to beat you at backgammon. Chess, too. And cards. Any game you choose. I'm as bored as you are."

He'd played enough with Darius, letting him win every time. It would be easier to not have to cheat that way, and plan the opponent's victory every time.

"Excellent. All my games are on that far shelf." Malory pointed to a corner of the vast, luxurious room.

Dare stayed where he was, looking at Malory's broken foot, the toes slightly red on the ends, the rest of it where it wasn't wrapped in soft cotton a funny shade of bruised yellow.

"Does it hurt?"

"The healers gave me essence of poppy. When I added my own glass of wine, to be honest I can't feel a thing." Malory grinned.

Dare let his smile widen.

Malory set his book aside on the satin counterpane. "If you want some wine, help yourself. There's meat and cheese and bread, too. And little cakes that taste of sweet and spice at the same time."

"But why did you call me to come here if your father hates—"

"Shut it."

Dare jerked back at the tone.

Malory gave him a pained look. "I don't want to talk about him. He doesn't have to know anyway. The guards are loyal to me and they brought you the roundabout way, didn't they?"

"Yes." Dare gripped his chain tight in his left fist.

"Good. What did you think of the murals?"

"They're amazing. We don't have murals like that in Brookfall. Or glorious sculptured walls like I have in my room, and like the ones in the throne room."

"No? What about secret passageways?"

"Yes, there are those, but they are dank and damp and ugly."

"Well, we Shastans do pride ourselves on our masters of the arts. I myself was taught to paint. I loved it, but I'm also terrible at it." He laughed.

Dare was not sure if he should laugh, too. With Darius, remarks like that were always a trap. If Darius ever thought Dare was laughing at him, he'd become angry for the rest of the day, and impossible to please, let alone get along with. Dare had learned how to make the days easy for both of them by curbing his behavior to suit Darius's twisted personality and bad moods.

"We are not taught art in Brookfall. Writing, yes, but only for reports, not fairytales. There are artists but they are self-made. All the art and sculpture in the castle there is ancient."

"All children like to make things, even out of dirt."

"Darius—uh, my servant and I—never played in the dirt."

"Hmph. I'm sure you didn't."

Dare turned away to the shelves. "Shall I select a number of games and bring them over?"

"Please. Since I can't easily get up."

Dare ignored the sarcasm in Malory's tone.

Malory continued, "I have crutches but I'm still getting used to them and the healers said for the first few days I'm to lie flat with my foot raised up."

Dare walked across the plush rugs. The room smelled fresh and airy despite its thick, shadowy décor. The brilliant shards of sunlight that shot in from the windows at random angles lit dust motes that made all of this seem, for a moment, like a dream.

Trying not to think of his position, his dishonesty, his life in the balance, Dare selected games that were his own favorites, the ones that were good distractions from his sheltered and sometimes cruel life with Darius. He set the games on the bed and moved a big chair to the side, sitting down and arranging his chain.

96

"You don't want wine?" Malory asked with an eyebrow raised.

"Maybe later."

They played chess first, then backgammon for hours, and Dare enjoyed himself, not even realizing that much time had passed until a servant brought lunch.

As the servant set things up, Malory got onto his crutches to go into the water closet. He would not allow Dare to help him at all, even when he nearly tripped.

Dare stood back and again could not help but compare Darius and Malory. Darius would have been all over him, leaning his full weight, taking pleasure when Dare struggled to please him. He might have even made Dare bring the chamber pot to him and hold his cock for him as he peed. With Darius, Dare could not predict the boy's strange habits even when they were five.

On crutches, Malory still looked exquisite, every bit of his royal blood revealed in his tall frame, the way he held his upper body, shoulders back, head raised. The way he moved even hobbling on crutches, as if he owned the world. His blond hair looked lit as if from within, brighter as he passed by the windows.

Dare looked hungrily at the food, but waited for Malory to join him before trying any of it.

When Malory returned, he said, "Well, that was fun. Trying to balance and pee."

Dare chuckled easier now around him. Darius, in the back of his mind, curled his lip.

Dare said, "I didn't realize it was time for lunch already."

"Thank you for staying."

He had never in his life been thanked for entertaining a prince.

Dare spent most of the day with Malory. The guards knocked on the door to check in a little too often. When Dare finally left to allow the prince some rest, he was taken back through the dark, secret passages of colorful artwork.

The next day, he woke to the same guard command.

"You are requested."

Eager to see Malory again—it staved off boredom for them both—he followed the guards. Seeing the torches light up the murals and frescos again made him wonder why it was all hidden.

"Why is all that beautiful art kept in the dark?" Dare asked Malory when they met again.

"No one knows why. And to have those walls moved into the light and the passageways dismantled would require too much time and effort, not to mention damage to the palace."

"That's too bad," Dare replied.

Days passed.

Every day, Dare visited Malory in his room. Every day, he grew more at ease around him, but the flutterings in his chest and stomach never ceased. They only grew stronger. He could no longer pass the feelings off as nerves. He wanted to hear that voice all the time. He wanted to watch the way Malory's face moved with his expressions, and to watch his eyes spark in delight at a quip or joke or funny story. He loved being in his presence, and his dreariest times were when he was escorted back to his own room alone for the night. In sleep, his bed felt too empty. He could never quite catch his breath.

*

One morning, Dare arrived to find Malory up on his crutches, dressed in soft black trousers, white shirt and gilt-edge waistcoat.

His figure tall and imposing, Malory may have been temporarily lame, but he still looked every inch a prince. His hair was wild as scattered light, locks of it uncombed, hanging against his cheek and covering one eye. Dare pictured frustrated servants struggling to get a comb through it for Malory's whole life.

Malory said, "I desperately need fresh air. The balcony just won't do. Will you come for a walk with me?"

"I'd be happy to, but can you make it that far?"

"Of course. You doubt me?"

Dare smiled. "Never. But what if the king sees. Hasn't he strictly forbidden us—"

"I don't care what my father says. If he sees us, I'll tell him the truth. That you play backgammon much better than my lordly friends, and I needed a challenge. I'll convince him a prince's company is what I need."

Dare grinned.

Malory wore one boot. His other foot was naked, the ankle carefully wrapped with long strips of white silk that probably offered more of a mental solace than actual physical support or comfort.

Malory must have been practicing with the crutches, for he took to the halls and the stairs with ease, making Dare's guards nervous as they hurried to keep up.

Once they were outdoors, Dare thought the wide palace steps, of which there were dozens, would look daunting to one on crutches. But Malory attacked them without complaint, never wobbling, steady as he made his way toward the trails through the poppies that led in various directions to the stables, the pond, and the castle gate where the healers' quarters and other outlying structures stood.

Today, white clouds skidded across the sky, and the wind was up. But still the sun shone. The air blew chill, but not cold.

Bask had insisted on coming along for the safety of Prince Malory, and held Dare's chain wrapped about his wrist, the end in his closed fist. Instead of walking beside Malory as he wished to do, Dare was forced to keep pace with the guard, who held himself back from the prince either from deference or habit of training, or both.

Darius had never liked walking or hiking or riding or anything to do with the outdoors. Even travel to the chateau had been a source of anxiety for him. But Dare loved sunlight and breezes and the scent of things blooming. He'd spent a lot of time in the Brookfall walled gardens, the only place Darius might deign to go mostly to chase and bully other servant kids.

Today the waters of the pond were the color of storms because of the cloud-cover. The white swans swam mostly at the far end, floating by the willows. Ornate, iron benches decorated the pond's edge.

Malory moved to one and sat, putting his crutches aside and wiping the back of his hand across his forehead.

"It's cool but I'm already sweating," he confessed. "Sit with me."

Bask had no choice but to stand in front of the bench holding Dare's chain so he could seat himself beside Malory.

Malory frowned. "Go away!" He waved his hand at Bask.

Bask said, "Yes, my lord, but I must make sure the prisoner is secured." He held up the chain.

"He's a hostage, not a prisoner."

Dare wondered at the difference.

"Give that to me!" Malory barked the order as if annoyed.

Bask gave the chain over to the prince, who took it lightly, placing his hand in his lap and snaking the chain over one thigh.

Dare felt a strange stirring deep within, as if Malory were holding a part of himself against his leg. As if they were touching. The chain had become that much of an extension of his body. He barely felt the collar anymore, except at night when he was trying to get to sleep. Then it might pinch and irritate. That was when he was reminded of the lie he was

100

living, the fabrication he maintained that had begun as a simple masquerade and now had become his very existence. A fate he had not asked for but now willingly wore like a uniform every day. His identity was not in question. He was no prince. But he must play the role for the sake of two kingdoms.

"What are you thinking?" Malory asked.

Dare glanced up, breaking his reverie. "What? Why?"

"You looked far away just now."

He blinked hard, feeling the wind on his cheeks, how it combed his hair back from his face. "I was thinking about the peace between our realms."

"Are you afraid your father will not keep it?"

"Sometimes."

"Are you worried about what will happen to you?"

"Yes, but I'm more worried about war. I saw too much bloodshed already when I was taken by your guardsmen. I don't want to cause more."

Brows gently furrowed, Malory contemplated him for a long moment. "I now realize the rumors of you I'd heard for years hold not one shred of truth to them."

Dare sighed. "I don't know what to do sometimes. I feel so useless. As if maybe my life is about to end."

"That won't happen."

"How do you know?"

"Because I'm the Shastan prince and I won't stand for it."

It had been stupid for Dare to ask the question. Of course Malory would have insight to his plight. Perhaps they never meant him harm. But he remembered the queen had wanted him in the stockade. She had not trusted him, and she was one-third in power here.

Dare worried his fingers in his lap, weaving them together. He stared over the vast pond, watching the reflections of the clouds in the water's surface. The trees and the meadow grasses bent a little in the breeze. The tall mountains to the northeast gleamed with snow at their highest peaks.

"You're always worried," Malory stated.

"Yes."

He leaned closer to him, almost whispering. "Dare. I am doing all I can to make people see you as a friend, not an enemy."

Dare turned to look at his honey-brown eyes. His voice came out thin and soft. "Thank you." His stomach clenched and his breath caught as Malory's mouth arched up in a gentle smile.

"You have been good to me these past days," Malory said.

"But of course. You were injured. It was my honor—"

Malory interrupted. "Not because of honor. Don't say that. It should be just because—because we are people, just people, and people sometimes find each other and keep company. Yes?"

Dare tilted his head. No one had ever said such words to him. He took a shallow breath, for his lungs were too tight now to hold much air. "Yes."

"Say it."

"Just because."

Malory smiled again, tender, and for a short time the entire world around them vanished and it was just the two of them sitting on a hard, black-iron bench, and nothing else existed, not ponds or swans or castles or wars. Not even princes.

Distantly, he heard a bell in a far-off tower. All he could think was, *This moment. It is ringing for this moment.*

Chapter Twelve

Dare could not imagine the real Prince Darius and Prince Malory married. What a farce that would have been. A tragedy.

Malory would not have put up with Darius's insolence for one second. He was strong-headed and firm, and would have smacked Darius's whining face without thought of insult. Darius would, of course, have attacked back. Their union—if it might ever have been called that—would have caused war, not peace. He was sure.

But it was Dare who played the prince now. Despite the collar, the label of "hostage" put upon him, and the fact that he was supremely hated by the queen and not at all respected by the king, he had power in his hands for once in his life. It was because, through sheer happenstance, the prince favored him.

He stared out the casement window.

The sky stretched gray today, the sun an obscured silver disk. The swans looked even more brilliant swimming lazy circles through the smooth steel waters of the pond. The meadows were still bright orange and white and yellow, and the trees dipped and swayed, the willows lapping at the shore's edge.

The temperature had dropped overnight in the early spring, winter's dance not quite finished after weeks of near-perfect weather. Though he missed the waterfalls of home, Dare loved the view out his window, both the palace grounds and what he could see stretching outward beyond the palace walls.

The expected knock came and he turned with a slow smile.

The chamber door opened. The guard merely beckoned now, for Dare knew what was expected of him. No more gruff, "You are requested" orders. This was now routine. He had already washed and dressed. The remains of his breakfast lay on his little wood table. He was ready.

When Dare arrived in Malory's quarters, the prince looked fine, dressed in blue, black and white. His winces and grunts of pain had reduced over the past couple of weeks. He still could not put weight on his right foot, but it did not seem to hurt as much every time he moved it from the pillow, or jostled it when he used the crutches.

Today, Malory sat at his table with his foot up on a pillow on a chair in front of him. In another prince's room not so long ago Dare would have been that chair, a footstool serving a lowly purpose. He would have knelt on hands and knees and stayed that way until ordered to rise.

Dare approached and saw the backgammon game set up. They grinned at each other in anticipation.

They played until Malory grew restless. "It really is more comfortable for me to be in the bed."

So they moved the game there.

For the first days, Dare used a chair at the side of the bed, but the bed was so big, he began sitting on the edge, with Malory's encouragement.

Now they both leaned against pillows, Dare on his stomach toward the foot of the bed, arms crossed over a cushion, and Malory against his headboard, with his bad foot sticking over the side so it touched nothing but air.

"Is it hurting you?" Dare asked.

Malory nodded. "More today, yes."

"Maybe it's because the weather is colder. I think it might rain. Weather affects joints. The older servants I knew always complained."

Malory smiled. "You always talk about the servants as if they are your friends."

He thought about that. Darius would never call a servant a friend. But Darius was not representative of princes, and certainly was not a good one.

"They are. Or rather were," Dare replied.

They played two more games, but Malory was restless, fidgeting with his pillows, and losing. Finally, his motions on the bed knocked and upset the backgammon board.

"I don't want to play anymore anyway," he said.

Dare put the game away and came back to the bed. He took liberty and sat by Malory's left side, his legs curled under him, his chain draped over the side.

"Is something bothering you? More than your ankle, I mean."

Malory's eyebrows looked sharp against his gold skin, darker than his blond hair. He shrugged and for a moment was silent, barely breathing.

Dare watched him, waiting, free to stare as he waited for Malory to find words to express himself, but using the time to admire the Malory's features, the high forehead dusted with brambly tangles, the cheekbones that cast his face in a pleasing, angular shape, and that broad mouth, the lips so pink, so soft.

Malory's eyes flashed nearly black in lamp and candlelight, but in outdoor sunshine they were truly the color of honey, and his gaze was the kind that swept people up. Or at least that was Dare's experience. He always felt like Malory was looking right through him and could see all his secrets brimming at once. It made his heart clench every time he told a lie.

When the silence became prolonged, Dare said, "You don't have to answer. It isn't my place to ask anyway."

Malory closed his eyes, his black lashes shining against his cheeks. He said, without opening them, "In a way it is your place to ask."

Dare frowned. "How so?"

"My father has arranged for me to marry a courtier of a rich lord. He says I'm too old to be unmarried and he insists."

"And you don't want—"

Malory interrupted. "It's arranged. I don't even know her."

"It's the way things are done. For gain, for purposes other than love."

Malory opened his eyes and that gaze looked right through Dare. Again. Always. "My father was trying to arrange for us to be married. Remember?"

"Of course I remember."

"If it had been sanctioned by your father, I mean, do you ever—"

"Think about it?" Dare finished for him. "Of course I do."

It wasn't Dare who might have married Malory, it was Darius, and that would have been a disaster. And, yes, Dare had thought of it. And wondered. For Malory had shown no aversion to the fact that the marriage would be between two men. His stomach fluttered deep inside at the thought.

"What were your thoughts about it?" Malory asked.

"I would have been honored." Both a lie and the truth. *He* would have been honored. The real Darius would not have felt the same.

Something like a smile shivered at the corners of Malory's mouth.

"What about you?" Dare asked.

"I hated the idea at first."

"Because of my reputation."

"You were a monster, they said."

Dare chuckled. "I know." *Oh, Darius.*

"But I didn't want to marry a woman, so I was intrigued."

"Not a woman?"

Malory shook his head.

106

"I understand maybe better than you think." Dare heard his voice drop. Soften.

"And now—" Malory stopped.

"And now?" Dare prompted. He desperately wanted to know what he was going to say next.

"Well, now my father is arranging my marriage to a woman." Malory shook his head. "At dinner last night we got into an argument."

That was not the statement Dare had been hoping for, but he kept his disappointment to himself. But then Malory surprised him.

"I got angry with my father because I would have rather the marriage be to a man. One time it might have been to you."

Dare's breath locked in his throat. He could only nod, stricken.

"I did not trust you at first."

You should not trust me now. But of course, other than the lie, Dare would never hurt Malory. Malory who made him feel hot and not quite put together inside. Who made him want things he had no right or place to want.

Aloud, he said, "But now I am a hostage of your country." He could not help the sad smile that firmed at his lips. He tried to shrug it off.

"Maybe your father will sign the treaty, make his promise and call for your return."

A sting of adrenalin pierced him at those words. He could not go back. His deception would be revealed. But he still managed to say, "Maybe."

"You sound unsure."

Dare sat very still, his hands clenched in his lap. He stared at them. Suddenly he felt feverish again. Sick.

"You aren't close at all?"

Dare shook his head.

"Would he forsake you?"

Danger flared from all sides. He'd stupidly allowed himself to forget that threat while entertaining the prince in his convalescence. If the truth was revealed, two kings would want him dead. If the truth was not revealed, two kings might still want him dead.

At an impasse, all he could do was wake every day and be amazed that he was still allowed to breathe. Malory had made him temporarily forget his immediate peril. The mask was as much a threat as it was momentary protection.

"If your father came round to his senses, if the proposal was put on the table again, what would you think?" Malory did not look at him as he spoke, but he rocked slowly forward, carefully adjusting the bandage on his ankle.

"I have told you I would not have objected." In every way, he had come to enjoy Malory, looking at him, talking with him, being with him. But the adrenalin of fear still coursed, making his skin prickle all over.

Light fell across the bed sharply, as if to stab at the sham of everything Dare was. He liked Malory too much, and looked forward to every day. But the lie slept within him, always threatening to wake.

The silver sky outside made sword shadows on the floor. A symbol of war. Of death.

"Dare," Malory said. He moved slightly in the bed.

Dare felt their thighs brush. He wanted to press back. *No.*

He let his head bow deeper, his hair falling against his cheeks, but hiding like that didn't work. He felt the palm against his jaw, warm and gentle. The weight on the bed shifted.

Malory's hair brushed his. His face was in front of him and the palm slid along his face until it was under his chin, lifting, pressing, bringing Dare's head up so their gazes met.

Glimmer of eyes. Honey brown sweetness. Nothing cruel or too needy in them as he was used to. This was simple openness. Affection.

Dare's mouth opened in amazement and Malory leaned in and kissed it with just the lips and a pressure that was enough to feel the softness of them without the teeth.

The high ceiling of the room, shrouded in wavering shadows from the flickering lamps, began to rotate. He closed his eyes, absorbing the sensation of the kiss as it melted throughout his body. Malory's presence, his wind-blown scent, and his warmth made Dare's body lose balance. He started to fall back, catching himself with his palm flat on the bed and hitting his chain, which rattled.

Malory's hand on his chin cupped him under the jaw and ear. A rush, like a storm, came over him, replacing all other sound. His skin tingled and an ache began between his legs, a feeling of euphoria, luck, fate all mixed together.

Dare wanted three things. Peace between their realms. To be free. And this kiss to last forever.

He was unsure he could ever have any of them. And the last? Malory deserved more than a lying, former prince's companion and servant.

The sudden thought punched him in the gut; dread tightened all his muscles. His body longed for Malory. His heart flew up as if never to come down again. He wanted him. While falling asleep, he thought of him. On waking, his first concern was for him.

But to continue his lie—this was not supposed to be a part of that. He was not supposed to get involved. Not supposed to fall in love. All he had wanted on that fateful day they were attacked by the Shastan guards was to keep breathing. To not have a sword plunged into his chest. That decision to keep being Prince Darius led to an idea of peace. But this? He could not allow the lie to extend into this.

He pulled back, gasping. "I—I can't."

Malory's breath huffed in his face, spicy, wine-scented. Dare wanted those lips back on his again, wanted to press up, reverent, gentle, taking care he did not nudge the injured ankle, but a slow fear threaded into his veins, pushing out the pleasure and replacing it with the shock of alarm. When revealed, if revealed, his lie would wound Malory far worse than any war. If he let this continue—

"You can," came a whisper. Malory leaned closer, again brushing his lips with his mouth, hot, alive.

Dare turned his head, muscles slow to obey, and breathed an anguished, "Please."

Malory took his hand away from his face, leaning back. "Why not? Don't you want—me?"

"It's not that. It's me. I swear it." Dare pulled himself away from Malory's side and stretched his legs over the side of the bed, sitting, his back to the prince.

"Dare—"

"It's not you. It's not you," Dare whispered.

"Then what is it?"

Dare got up, swaying, the metallic light from all the windows blinding him, and the idea that maybe he was dreaming taunted him. But he knew everything around him was really happening.

The day was so gray and everything so quiet.

"I'm sorry. I didn't mean push you." Malory spoke as if from far away.

That rush in his ears came again, but not from pleasure this time. Fear.

"Dare, what is it? You can tell me."

Dare shook his head, eyes tightly closed. He let out a heavy breath and moved toward the door. He had to leave. Get away from Malory and think.

"Don't leave." Spoken from behind him.

But Dare needed solitude. For what, he did not know. To scream, maybe. To break things. To cry.

Everything had changed too fast. The death of Darius. The rebirth of Darius. What had he been thinking?

He could say the real Prince Darius had ordered him to go on with his role. Be the prince. But who would believe him? It was his word alone. The word of a liar.

110

He needed to go back to his room.

Dare took another step toward the door. His chain dragged.

"Please, don't go. I'm sorry. I didn't mean anything. It's just what you said about the marriage and—and I got carried away. I couldn't help it."

Another step. He was almost at the door. He could reach out now and touch it. Leave behind this fine nest of velvets and warmth and the embrace of a beautiful prince.

"Dare. Please!"

He put his palm on the handle, feeling the cold iron move up his arm.

"Dare."

He opened the door and walked through it, seeing Hoop there and handing him his chain.

As he closed the door behind him, he heard Malory, trapped on the bed by a broken ankle, still calling. "Dare! Dare!"

"Back to my rooms, please," Dare said.

This time, moving through the secret passage, he did not see any beauty or color on the walls, only the fading light-to-dark straight ahead of him. He felt only the dead weight of his heart in his chest.

Chapter Thirteen

The heavy door opened with an empty scraping noise.

Dare did not look up or turn around. He sat before his uneaten breakfast, staring at the rain as it made tracks down the window.

Behind him, today the voice was Bask's. "You are requested."

"Tell him no. It is the king's order I not see him and you know it."

Bask said, "Prince Malory too often does not follow the king's orders. He is favored that way."

"I said no."

He heard the door shut, a weighted thunk.

Dare had not slept much, and when he did his slumber came in fitful increments during which he jerked himself awake, then fell back into a kind of numb distance. He had not screamed or cried or broken a single thing.

His mind kept trying to solve the problem. His heart wrenched in denial. For there was no solution. None. He could play the role out and probably eventually be caught and die. Or he could reveal himself and most certainly face the executioner's block.

Over and over, he wondered what it might be like to die. To feel the sword through heart or head or neck. To feel that moment of bright pain unlike anything the imagination could define.

He'd watched Darius die, seen the torture of it in his eyes, the betrayal. And so much blood. He hated blood. That scene kept playing in his mind, as if it were a dream. He'd smelled the sour-metal blood scent for days afterward, felt the way it had stiffened the sleeves of the red velvet coat he wore on the way to Shastan.

His fever had blocked his thoughts for a lot of that journey, bringing a strange reprieve despite the pain of his illness. He had thought he might die. Now he realized everything would have been easier if he had.

He listened to the tapping of the rain, erratic like his pulse, the sky weeping, the world losing all color, the air harder to breathe.

He used to like the rain. Today there was nothing to like about its harsh beauty, its insistence on making everything into an immeasurable cave, as if he and the whole world were inside a giant sword ready only for cold killing, for violence, for blood.

He was that sword but with no control. He would be wielded. Used. The tool between the world of the living and the world where he now sat. Prince Darius. Played by the servant. The worst monster rumors could ever tell tales of. But he couldn't even get that part right.

*

Prince Darius had foretold that this time would come when he was dying.
When he said to Dare: *Well, be me. I don't care. But you'll find out what it's like. Everything will go wrong for you. You'll see.*

Darius had been worse than a brat, but was always blunt with the harsher truths. The way he saw the world was not necessarily wrong, but not always right, either.

Until now, he'd believed Darius's view of the world had been as if he continually looked through his own mask of dark, labyrinthine vision. But maybe it wasn't a mask, but more a purity of seeing, clear but without hope. Clarity might well have been one of Darius's talents, dark and depressing as it was.

As the day drew in a thousand damp breaths, no one bothered Dare except the servant girl who came with his lunch. Which he did not eat.

He let the fire die behind the grate of his hearth, though there was plenty of kindling and logs.

Toward evening, his door opened again. Expecting more food to avoid, he saw Hoop standing in the dimness of the hall light.

"You are requested." Gruff.

Dare stood and walked to the window. "No." He placed one hand on a cold pane, square and framed in black metal.

In his mind he saw Malory, like him, sitting in the tarnish of the day, wondering what he had done wrong.

His lips pressed tight at the memory of that warm kiss. His first friend. His first love. And he'd had to lie to get it.

His body drenched itself in the heated memory. It had been two kisses, actually, the second promising so much more even though it was a mere brush of plush skin to skin. The space between them had been filled with sparks enough to make the whole room swelter.

"He said not to ask you, but to order you."

Dare turned to face him, the hotness on his body going cold. "Tell him I am ill."

"I am to drag you to him if I must. Those were his words."

Dare had no doubt Hoop would do just that, or carry him if he had to. He was a hulk of a man. It would be nothing to him but an unpleasant chore.

Hoop came into the room, looking around. "Why is it so cold in here?"

"I didn't notice."

Hoop said, "You are an odd hostage princeling, aren't you?" He picked up Dare's shining chain and gave a rough tug.

Dare stumbled but went with him. He had some pride left, enough not to want to be dragged or carried.

*

The room swam with heat.

Malory sat on a blanketed couch before a roaring fire. The violently burning logs drowned out the tumbling and tapping rain on the windowpanes, the balcony, and the double doors. Malory's right foot, draped with clean, white silk, was propped on a low stool. A footstool.

He looked up, dark gaze on an expressionless face.

Hoop shoved Dare through the doorway, and threw his chain down. It chimed as it hit the floorboards between the rugs. The door shut with a *thunk* behind him.

Dare could feel his heart, the beat tight in his throat, burning through his body. He stood very still, looking at Malory.

Shame and fascination warred within him. For Malory, despite his injury, filled the space with his essence, his power that was more than princehood. More than kingdoms and treaties and wealth. The intense features, that flaxen hair like knots of gold, the regal line of his posture. All of it seemed to bend toward Dare, the spirit of him, the closeness they'd both felt these last weeks. It was more than heat. It was possibility. Connection. An elixir of gravity from which Malory was the source. It encircled him, traveled around him like a wind escaped from a far off door to the sun left open.

Where Dare was dark, Malory was golden in every way, light coming to feast upon the bleakness he had never fully realized surrounded his being since he was five years old. Always he'd denied the shadows. Even Darius could not make him blind to the beauties in life, to the light. But now Malory made him realize he'd never entered that state of being. Until now.

Now when he was a hostage.

Now when he probably did not have long to live.

Now when everything Malory thought Dare was came from a lie.

"Please come and sit with me. That's all I ask," Malory said. His face still showed nothing.

The fire danced and fought with itself behind a gleaming, silver grate.

Dare's chain dragged. He sat at the far end of the red couch on velvet cushions, propped by velvet pillows. He draped his white-shirted arm over the edge.

Malory watched him the whole time, the dark sharp eyes not cold despite the shifting in them but hot hot hot. He may not have asked more from Dare in words—"just sit with me"—but whatever was between them asked for more, for everything. Demanded it. The space between them lived with an entity of their creation called longing, need, adoration.

"I just want you to know," Malory said, voice low, rumbling over the sounds of the fire. "You can tell me anything."

"That's why you made me come back?"

"Aren't we friends?" Malory asked.

Slowly, Dare nodded. Malory responded with a pained smile. "I would keep your secrets to the grave," he said.

Dare let out a sound of disbelief. "You barely know me."

"Is that so true?"

"Yes."

"Let me tell you what I do know, then." He leaned forward and picked up his chalice but did not bring it to his lips. He stared into the liquid depths. "I know you are honorable. You have a gentle nature. You are kind."

Dare leaned back, raising his hand so that his elbow rested on the couch's arm.

"Everyone defers to royalty. Honesty is not a trait we know." Dare rarely made speeches. This one came out of him in a rush of words. He barely heard himself, but he couldn't stop. "Servants tell you you look fine when you are a mess. Companions let you win your games. Politicians tell you what they think you want to hear to gain ground. Courtiers look to fatten their purses and spice their beds. What makes you think I'm anything less than deceitful myself? What makes you think I am not focused on my own agendas? That I, for one moment, am anything that you see before you?"

"Because you have nothing to lose anymore," said Malory. "So you have no agendas, no deceit."

"I have my life, still."

Malory breathed in hard. "I'm not finished. Because of how we've connected lately—and you cannot deny it, I don't think you're being deceitful. This is real. And anyway, as long as we're asking each other the hard questions now, what makes you think I can't smell deceit and lies a mile away? I'm not stupid. Authenticity is rare. The court is all games and glamour. I'm not some naïve child."

"Of course not. I didn't mean—" Dare stopped, biting the inside of his lower lip. Did he mean he could smell Dare's own deceit?

Despite the warmth of the room, his skin felt chilled. Maybe it had been the walk through the secret passageway where no heat reached. Maybe the dank air there had sent its chilly fingers under his clothing, fingers that grasped and would not let go. He pushed himself further into the cushions.

"Dare,"

"Mal—"

They both spoke at the same second. The firewood popped and snapped. Dare saw the whirl of firelight in Malory's ruby chalice.

"What were you going to say?" Malory asked.

"The—the friendship between us. I did not mean to give the impression I have faked that. That I pretended—" His voice trailed.

"Exactly what I was saying." Malory shifted. "But there is something you seem to think will come between us. I can feel it. Is it more than just that our realms are enemies? You want to tell me. At least I think you do."

Dare winced. How did Malory know these things?

"I can't."

Malory let out a pained laugh. "Maybe you're in love with another."

It was such a bold statement. Dare's head jerked up in shock. "If only it was that simple."

"I think this closeness between us, well, it isn't frivolous. I'm not good at saying these things, but if you told me anything, anything at all, I'd listen."

"Yes, I'm sure you'd take it to the grave. But not this." Dare felt himself go even colder. "Not this thing. You have no clue."

"You insult me?"

"No. Just telling the truth. You should use your powers to see there is no deceit in that statement."

Malory rolled his eyes. "Now you have me even more intrigued."

Dark winced. "Just don't ask anymore."

"I could have it tortured out of you."

Dare looked up in time to see the teasing glint in those beautiful eyes. But Dare did not smile. "Why don't you? I've been threatened with the dungeon-master more than once."

Malory shifted closer to him, looking him up and down. "I don't care what your secret is. Not really. Except for the fact that it made you walk out on me yesterday. And that it has been keeping you from me today."

"You should care."

"I don't want us to stop being what we were, friends, just because of yesterday. I don't want that to happen."

"So you ordered me to come back."

"Yes."

"Are you ordering me to be your friend?"

"I thought we already were."

Now Dare saw the hurt flash, blue-white, in Malory's eyes. That lost look stabbed at his gut.

Malory added, "You'll have to say it to my face if it's not true."

"I'm sorry," Dare said. "It is true. We are friends. But I—I just wish things were different."

Now Malory pulled his leg from the footstool, bringing his injured ankle up to the couch so that he could scoot closer to Dare.

"I've made you my promise. To protect you. To protect even your secret. What more can I do? I'm a prince and so are you. Do you want me to bow down to you?"

"No!"

"I will."

"Stop it."

"Damn my ankle, I will go to my knees. Dare, you're the best thing that's happened to me in a long time. I love being with you. Haven't you enjoyed it?"

"Of course I have!"

"A prince does not bow to another prince. But I would to you, Dare. Doesn't that mean anything to you?"

But I am no prince. Dare's eyes began to sting. He had not expected this. He had not planned for this at all. Getting to know the prince and entertain him was supposed to be like his time with Darius, shallow, no expectations, just existing from day to day trying to distract himself from his situation.

He played a prince now, but his situation had not improved. Being royal meant only that he kept his life, nothing more. The clothes might be nice, but he'd had nice clothes with Darius, even if very few. And though he'd slept on a pallet at the foot of Darius's bed, it had been soft and clean and he had access to as many pillows as he wanted.

He caught his breath hard. He didn't mean for the gasp to come out so loud.

Malory leaned toward the table, poured wine into a chalice and brought it to him.

"Here. Drink."

Dare's stomach rebelled at the thought. He hadn't eaten all day.

"Come on. It'll help."

Dare took another breath, blinking against the sudden tears.

Rain and rain and rain today. Everywhere.

Dare took the wine and drank a small sip. Hand shaking.

He'd never met anyone like Malory before. The court at Brookfall ignored him. The servants he'd known who were nice to him stayed clear because no one wanted to get in the way of Prince Darius and his unpredictable temperament. He did not, however, feel he'd lived an isolated life. He attended public banquets in the place of Prince Darius. He was afforded the education and training of a prince. Even the fashion. But now he realized how alone he'd really been. A mere tool of a spoiled boy.

"Take another sip," came the gentle voice at his side.

He obeyed.

"Better?"

It wasn't, but he nodded.

"I want to know what has you so upset. Was it just the kiss?"

Dare nearly sloshed the wine over the edge of his cup. "No. That was—that was wonderful."

Malory's lips pressed tight, holding back a smug smile.

Dare couldn't look at him without wanting him. He shut his eyes hard.

"No harm will come to you in this room. I promise."

Dare got up from the couch, holding his wine, and approached the paned glass doors to the balcony. The rain drops came down hard, spattering off the wooden deck and shooting upwards, only to fall again. Everything was shiny but bleak. Beyond the balcony a gray mist shrouded the grounds. It was like being adrift in clouds.

120

As Dare became lost in the blurring of the world, a part of his mind, as if left behind in a distance he could not see, manifested. The true part of him, the heart. The part of him that resided in the still-pure state of believing in goodness, beauty, hope. Purpose.

He heard his voice, toneless, hesitant. "If I reveal myself to you, I know you will hate me."

"Try me."

Dare leaned his forehead against the cold glass. He was glad not to be facing Malory as he spoke. "It is true that Prince Darius was a monster."

The words choked him, his throat tight.

"Go on."

Dare swallowed hard. "The rumors you told me about—they're fairly accurate."

Dare heard a chuckle.

"But you're not like that at all," Malory said.

"I know."

"Then why do you say this?" asked Malory.

"Because it's still true; the monster that he was lived. The spoiled prince who despised everything and everyone, who did not get along with his father, and hated social events, hated the world, hated everything, really."

"I don't understand. Why are you talking about yourself in the third person?" Malory asked.

"I just told you. He hated social events. Anything public. People. Travel. All of it. He was spoiled. He never did anything he didn't want to do. Spiteful, he fought every aspect of being a prince. Of even being a good person."

"You're a good person," Malory argued. "Stop talking like that. Like you're two people."

Dare turned to face the couch and the sparkling fire, the flames blue and orange as they burned lower. He did not look at Malory. "I can't stop."

"What? What do you mean?"

"Two people. Two princes. One who was a real prince. And one who wasn't but looked a lot like him, was made to be his companion and take his place at public events the prince did not want to attend. At first the prince needed a double if there might be danger from things like assassination or kidnapping attempts, but later he used his companion to attend functions just to spare him from his hatred of dealing with people, and what was for him the agonizing boredom of a prince's duties."

"What are you saying?"

"Two boys. There were two boys. Both named Darius. Both living in the same room. Both almost identical. One a prince. One the prince's companion."

"I don't see how this has anything to do with—"

"You're not listening to me."

"I heard every word."

In his peripheral vision, Dare saw Malory sit up straighter and turn his head as if thinking back on these past weeks, re-assessing.

"I am not the real Prince Darius."

Silence.

"My betrayal began when your Shastan guards killed everyone in our traveling party, saying they only wanted the prince. The real Darius, dressed as a servant, died in my arms. I thought they would kill me if they knew he was dead, so I played the part. So I could live."

Dare glanced toward Malory. He could see only his profile, face tilted down as if staring at the red and pink woven rug before the fire. Hair glistening in the flame-light.

The rain whipped up. A wind pushed against the panes of the windows and the balcony doors with a begging whine to be let in.

When Malory said nothing, Dare shut his eyes only to feel tears drop onto his cheeks, burning. He was not sure how long he stood there, hearing the storm, feeling the sting on his cheeks, and the heaviness of his collar and chain against his trembling throat. Only when he heard a tapping on the rug near his feet did he open his eyes to see Malory balanced on one crutch, right ankle raised, standing a mere hand-span from him.

Malory reached out with his free arm and grabbed Dare by the shoulder, fingers clenching, nearly bruising.

"You lied to me?"

"I did not mean to betray you." Dare's voice shook and he wanted to draw back.

Eyes dark, but silver in their depths reflecting the sodden day, Malory brought his eyebrows together as if in pain. He pushed Dare a little with his hand, still clutching him.

"You can never tell anyone this." Malory's voice came out roughened, overly loud.

Dare swiped the back of his hand across his damp face.

Malory squeezed harder. "Say it. You won't. Not ever! No matter what!"

"I won't." His voice shook. He couldn't breathe right.

"Promise!'

"I won't! I promise!" Destruction ruled his veins, and inside his chest and mind. Malory was ordering him. Firm. Angry. How Malory must hate him now.

"Good. Because if you do, I don't know if even I can save you."

"Save me?"

"You're more the prince than the actual prince was, by the way you tell this story."

Confused, Dare shook his head. "But I have no royal blood in my veins."

"It doesn't matter. You're him now. The Prince of Brookfall. Prince Darius. No one will ever know what you just said. Do you hear me? Do you understand? Because I can't save you otherwise."

"I—I—" Dare had no more words. Had Malory just spoken of saving him a second time?

"You have to be him. You have to."

The hand on Dare's shoulder hurt. He let out a soft groan but did not pull away.

"Dare, this is your life and I won't see it taken. I made you a promise."

Dare's eyes welled up again. He shook his head. "Of course I would not hold you to it."

"But don't you see? I don't want to lose you. You're the best—" He stopped, took a breath. "The best thing that's ever happened to me. We're going to make an accord. And then we will work together to save the realms, to rule. And most of all, to keep you alive."

Shocked, Dare almost fell to his knees. "Your Highness—"

"No. Don't. Don't do that. Here in these rooms use my name."

"You must despise me, though. I thought you would despise me, but you want me to live even after what I told you?"

The hand on his shoulder loosened, let go. It came up to touch his face, wiping at his cheek, cupping it.

"I do not despise you. With you it is the very opposite." Malory paused, gulping. "I know you felt it, too."

Dare's jaw trembled.

"Say yes, you felt it, too," Malory prompted.

Almost a whisper. "Yes." He lowered his eyes, feeling lower than the servant he'd just revealed himself to be. Lower than a footstool.

Malory's hand against Dare's cheek forced him to look into his eyes. "You are the prince of Brookfall. Say it."

"But it's different now," Dare began.

"Say it."

"I am the prince of Brookfall." His words came out meek.

"Stronger. Again."

"I am the prince of Brookfall." His voice had resonance to it now.

"There it is. And no one will ever say differently from now on."

"But—but I can never go home. The servants, the courtiers and the king will know me." His face, stiff in his agony, ached. "The public would not, but I can't risk it at the castle."

"Then we will take pains to have you rule from elsewhere when the time comes."

"But I could never rule."

"You are the prince of Brookfall," Malory said firmly. "This will be our pact from now until the ends of our lives."

His breath came hard and fast, wisping into Malory's face. He pictured himself damp-faced and scared, in-drawn and unsure, certainly not the image of a future ruler.

Malory peered at him; he showed no anger in his features, only a strangely desperate will.

"Agreed?" Voice low, demanding.

Dare nodded slowly.

"Say it."

"I agree." His voice sounded like a far off whisper.

But so many hurdles existed for the plan to fail. Dare had only taken this disguise temporarily. He'd never expected to keep it forever. Day to day in Shastan he'd awakened and played the princely role, rarely thinking further ahead. He had thought eventually he would be returned to Brookfall where he'd meet his fate at the hand of the king, hoping the king might allow him to live because he'd been Prince Darius's only friend.

His only other best case scenario was that he might escape with the jewels he'd been wearing when he'd been taken, and start a new life somewhere on the streets of Shastan.

Never had he aspired to pretend to actually rule a country, though during his years with Darius he understood he would be expected to "double" for him throughout his lifetime. But to actually rule? No.

"No matter what, this is our pact," Malory said.

Shaky, Dare repeated, "This is our pact."

For a prolonged moment, they stared at each other. Then Malory glanced to the side of Dare's head and moved his fingers up and through this hair.

Malory said, softly, as if their previous conversation had been abruptly forgotten, "I've never seen hair so shining and dark as yours."

Every part of Dare's body warmed, and his skin shivered with an inner liquid joy.

He kept thinking, *But I am only a servant.*

But it was as if Malory had imbued him with privilege, rank and honor by the very power of his princehood. *You are Prince Darius. Say it!*

Kings and queens gave knighthoods, bestowed high titles, but never that of the level of king or queen itself except through marriage.

Malory leaned closer, using his crutch and Dare for balance, and brushed his lips across Dare's. Their third kiss in two days. This was what Dare had been trying to avoid. This was what Dare wanted but could not initiate.

Now he allowed Malory to lean against him, and Dare pushed himself into the kiss, his lips like embers, his mouth opening. Even as his mind said this was impossible, his body could not deny he'd wanted Prince Malory from the moment they'd met.

Everything pressed soft and hard at once. The air like velvet, the caressing heat of the hearth fire, the way the tapping hum of the rain cocooned them in its edgeless, liquid sound. Malory's feral hair brushed against Dare's forehead, the tangles pliant, silken where he expected rough or crisp.

Dare lifted his arms and the soft cloth of Malory's robe brushed his wrists and the backs of his hands. But the chest

126

that crushed against his, and the hips—all hard. And lower—urgent pressure in the tented shapes of their trousers.

The kiss deepened. He was being dishonest to continue this role even with Malory's staunch support, and yet this pact between them, and the resulting kiss was the most pure and honest thing he'd ever done.

Their tongues met in the briefest of touches. Malory pulled back.

"Damn! I missed you. You walked out and I knew that couldn't be the end."

Dare leaned his forehead against Malory's. "Now you know why."

"You have to stay. Today. And you have to come to me every day."

Dare felt his mouth turn up. "I will." Tremors passed through his body, hot, so hot.

"And then we'll figure out the problem of you being held hostage. I swear, I will solve it. I'll make my father see. We'll make him see. That you're here now to better things between our realms. As an ally."

"I am an ally. Even the real prince—" He gulped. Malory had said never speak of it again. But he had to say. "Even Darius, as mad as he was, did not really want war. It was a joke to him. He wouldn't even know how to begin to manage one."

"That's why kings have advisors. To manage everything for them."

"But he wouldn't have cared about anything like that. He would have stayed in his rooms in the dark yelling at every servant or ordering them whipped, wanting only to play at children's games, appearing at court purely to despise and dismiss all around him."

"You lived with him all those years. How?"

Dare pressed his lips to the side of Malory's mouth.

"I think I'm the only one he almost ever liked. I am the one person who tried to help him, make him feel better.

Everyone else endured him, and then ran. Even the king treated him like an unwanted necessity, protecting him and indulging him but never showing love."

"It sounds—awful." Malory moved so their lips connected once more.

Dare's hands were flat on Malory's back now, one over each shoulder blade, feeling the curve of muscle and bone through the velvet robe. What would it be like to touch him skin to skin?

It only took the thought to send a thrill chasing through his system.

The taste of Malory was wine and spice. Every delicate scent whirled to arouse him. The room smelled of moss, rivers, burning oak. Dust on velvet. Salt of lust.

What do shared secrets smell like? *This,* Dare thought. *And this.*

Before he realized it, he was helping Malory to the bed.

He had started out as support for one prince on his hands and knees, but now he was standing, supporting the weight of another, and this time he wanted to. This time he wanted to wrap around Malory until he could not tell one of their bodies from the other.

They sat on the edge of the bed at the same time, Malory giving a small groan, reaching around Dare, kissing him again and again. They fell into the pillows and Dare laughed into Malory's kiss, going deeper; their tongues danced. Malory's hands on his face had wiped away all sign of tears that had fallen just minutes ago.

The bed smelled of lavender and was soft as a cloud. Saffron light flickered about them on the walls and the silk bed-curtains and the rich blues of the counterpane. The rain-shadows were silver and gray.

The kisses colored Dare's mind in wing-shapes of copper and red. He had never felt this way in his life. Like his world was only beginning. New and fresh and clean.

Malory lifted the shirt from Dare's trousers and ran his hands up under it. Dare's skin went tight all over his body.

In turn, he reached up and untied the ribbon at Malory's throat, parting the dark robe and pushing it back from his broad shoulders. The bronze chest gleamed, outlined in thick black material, muscular. Dare leaned back from their kiss and looked, then touched with the flat of his palm, running fingertips over the ridges of ribs. Silk over marble. Beauty in lean, hard grace. He wanted to put his mouth on that chest. He wanted to taste it.

Malory gave a sudden wince and let out a sound of frustration.

"Your ankle," Dare said. "Lie back and I'll put a pillow under it."

Malory half-obeyed, lying on his back and propping himself on his elbows as he watched Dare gently lift his leg and place the foot on the softest pillow he could find. The ankle was thickly wrapped in clean white silks around and around to support it. Even with that, it needed not to be jostled.

Dare crawled back up to the head of the bed and leaned over Malory.

"All right?" he asked.

"Everything is all right," Malory answered. "I want everything with you."

Dare let himself touch Malory's hair right then, expecting a sensation of bristly grass, but despite the crazy patterning of the pale strands mixing curls with clumps and errant patches of straight locks, it was like putting his hand on a skein of the softest yarn.

"You are untamed," he said softly.

"An observation my mother has made many times." Malory grinned.

Dare looked down at the golden-ness of the prince where the robe fell back all the way past his flat stomach. He imagined embracing him skin to skin would be like holding fire. Sharp and hot. Like capturing the sun.

"I have had lovers look at me many ways," Malory observed. "But never the way you're looking at me now."

"How?"

"As if you are dreaming awake."

"Maybe I am." Dare smiled.

Malory lifted his arms, still slightly trapped in the sleeves of his robe. Dare went into the embrace, shirt out and rucked up, hair falling onto his forehead. Every kiss between them made a new storm of Dare's feelings.

Outside, the rain had let up a little, but not the mist, which was silver against the windows in the flickering of the oil lamps.

A hand breached the waistband of Dare's trousers, working past the tightness, fingertips brushing the curve of his ass. All need centered between them and Dare brought his hands under Malory's shoulders, pulling their bodies tightly together.

Finally they came to a point where the clothing impaired them too much.

In soft tones, they each communicated gentle demands. "Lift up." "Stretch back." "Push down." Their voices were like a song in the chrysalis of the room, whispers and low tones, but filling the air with a deep yearning.

They could not undress each other quickly enough. Malory's robe was easiest to manage, for beneath it he wore only the softest of white muslin sleeping trousers which, after the drawstring was untied, came off in a moment as they took care not to tug at his right foot.

Dare had a waistcoat, and laces down the front as well as at the edges of his puffy, white sleeves. His trousers fastened with button flaps that stuck. They laughed as their fingers collided when they both tried to undo them at once.

Dare's boots were also a problem, with lots of buckles up to the knees.

When the clothes were heaped on the rug by the bed, Dare stretched on his side, up on his elbow, leaning over the burning magnificence that was Malory. He was all limbs, it seemed, with slim hips and waist, but well-defined muscles in his shoulders and arms. And, well, he was copper and bronze everywhere, from the gold hair at his head to the sheen of his skin all the way to his toes. His cock, too, was of dark gold, almost brown, and fully hard, with a firm foundation of two, tight round balls dusted lightly in gilt-colored hair.

Dare gasped.

Malory gripped Dare's upper arm and lifted himself partway up, careful of his foot. "Let me see you."

Dare sat back on his heels, then crouched over Malory, a knee outside each of Malory's thighs, and lifted up. When he saw Malory's gaze sweep over him, his own cock hardened even more, jerking a little where it jutted upwards toward his belly. He loved that Malory looked at him, the attention of it, hoping he did not disappoint. He felt ready to come before they'd even started.

Malory placed both hands on Dare's hips, light and warm, holding him steady. "You're gorgeous, my prince."

Dare flushed all over. *Prince.* Even in private, all secrets revealed, Malory was going to call him that?

Dare lowered his palms to Malory's chest, running them back and forth over the hard muscles, fingertips brushing taut nipples.

Hands moved from Dare's hips to his ass, caressing. "Move up," Malory said. "I want to taste you."

He felt the tip of his cock flare at the hungry command. He leaned down, kissed Malory deeply, then started to lift up and move forward when a loud bang sent a shock of cold through the room. On his hands and knees, Dare jerked his head around and saw the royal chamber door fly open and two burly guards stomp over the threshold.

Dare dropped to the far side of the bed behind Malory, giddy, dizzy as if his heart had stopped. He pulled a part of the bedcover up to his belly.

Malory sat straight up at the waist not even bothering to cover himself, or stop the loud growl that emitted from his throat.

"How dare you enter here without knocking. Get out! Now!" he shouted.

"King's orders," said Hoop. "Prince Darius, the traitor, is to come with us now."

Both guards shifted on their feet, even big Hoop who took no nonsense from anyone. They kept darting glances at Malory's nudity, then looking away.

"He's not a traitor, he's a hostage. And I have ordered him to be here with me as my companion in my convalescence. So get out before I order you both flogged!"

"The king commands it. He is to come immediately."

"You are being impertinent. What is the reason behind this? Tell me or get out now!"

"An act of war has been committed by the king of Brookfall. Prince Darius is no longer a hostage, but a prisoner of war. His life is forfeit, should the king decree it. He is to be taken to the dungeon to await trial."

Chapter Fourteen

Dare watched Malory's mouth drop open, then close again as if he tried to speak but couldn't.

"Get dressed, Prince Darius, and come with us," Hoop ordered.

Embarrassed at his state of arousal, Dare climbed over the bed and dropped to the floor to gather his clothes. He quickly put on his trousers and shirt.

Malory found his voice again. "He does not need to be taken to the dungeon. He can wait in his chamber under guard!"

"King's orders," Hoop repeated.

"That makes no sense! He's a prince."

"Your Highness, you must talk to your father."

"You do not treat royalty this way, even a royal hostage!"

"I'm sorry, Your Highness. There are more guards waiting outside."

Dare's hands shook as he buckled his boots. Where only seconds ago his body was flushed and alive, now a deep cold coursed through him. Not only that, they'd been caught in such a private moment. And there were more guards waiting outside. Would they decide to tell the king?

He could not look at Malory. If he did, he knew he would lose all control, all will. Break down.

A million thoughts went through his mind at once. He could make sense of none of them except obeying the guards, doing as the king of Shastan commanded.

At his side, he saw a dark shape and realized that Malory, once again clad in his velvet robe, had slid from the bed onto his good foot. He leaned against the bedpost to support his weight. He said to Dare, "I will get dressed and accompany you."

Before Dare could answer, Hoop said, "You should not to be seen with the enemy prince. You were never supposed to have any contact with him. If you accompany us, I will most certainly be punished."

"I don't care! You can't do this. You can't take him to the dungeon! I won't have it, and if you disobey me, I'll order you all flogged!"

Dare glanced up, seeing the pain across Malory's features. Softly, "I'll go. It's all right. I'll go. Talk to your father. That's how you can help me."

Dare stood up, heading for the door, chain dragging across the rug and the wood. The room had gone cold. The fire in the grate winked in glowing embers. Outside, the rain began to pour, hard as hailstones.

"No!" Malory ran forward, as if forgetting his injured foot. "You have no right! No right! I am your prince!" As his harsh words echoed in the big room, his ankle gave out. He fell, catching himself against the doorframe, slowly sliding down it. His dark robe pooled around him.

Dare turned, wanting to run to him, but a firm grip fastened on his upper arm and Hoop dragged the chain up from the floor, pulling roughly. "Umph, you're not getting away. Come on."

There were three more guardsmen in the hall.

Hoop slammed the prince's chamber door shut, cutting off the angry growls of Malory.

Dare almost lost his balance as they led him a different way. No secret passageways this time. He was going out, away from the palace, and down the hill to the dark, walled prison. The king's dungeon. The place he thought he'd be sent to from the beginning.

He tried to get his bearings, keep control. But he couldn't even swallow, his throat was so dry. His voice, had he cared to use it, was lost. He wanted to fight; he wanted to weep. But mostly he wanted Malory not to cause trouble for himself just because of him. Therefore, he would do everything the guardsmen told him to do. Obey every order from the king.

Down two flights and they were in the grand foyer, all marble columned and checkered floors, unicorn statues and fountains, tall blue ceilings and ornate double doors.

Outside, when they came out from under the ornate, arched portico, rain slashed Dare's eyes and face. His shirt became instantly drenched. The world was a silver haze of cold indifference. It did not care about men's fates. It never had.

He did not protest his fate aloud, but inside he was crying out. It was difficult to put one foot in front of the other as they scrambled through puddles and mud along the pathway framed by long wet grass and orange flowers.

The walls about the dungeon were taller than the building, but through the iron-bar gates Dare could see the long structure, and he suspected from tales of Brookfall's own dungeon (which he'd never been in) that it went down and down many levels into darkness and an underworld of horrors he could only imagine.

The rain was fierce and cold. The big metal gates screeched on their hinges. They smelled of rust and sharpness. Through the whirls of water, he could barely see the yard that led to the entrance. The guards pulled him, stumbling along. The ground was slippery, the rock-lined path a river.

They went up cobbled, stone steps, some crumbling from age. The broken parts showed veins of blue and green and the roughness looked almost pretty where the rain wet them, making them shine.

But there was nothing pretty about this place. The building itself was gray brick cloaked in mist, square with guard towers at the four corners that poked through the fog like dark fangs. An armed guard stood on either side of the steps.

Squinting, Dare could see the doors at the top, black metal, featureless, set in iron framework. He could not see windows anywhere but as he got closer he saw all across the front of the building, low grates. Those would be for air, he thought, and what little light might leak through to each cell beneath those grates. Cells in the middle of the dungeon, or on deeper levels, might never get any outside light or fresh air at all.

The storm blew a cold wind along Dare's drenched body, but that wasn't why he had begun to shiver uncontrollably.

The guards shoved him toward those thick, ominous double doors. One of them banged his fist on the metal, and Dare heard echoing booms within. The place sounded deep.

A small, rectangular door squeaked open at eye level, and two gray eyes peered out. "Who goes?"

"The king's new prisoner."

The mysterious man behind the door gave a rude grunt and slammed the tiny door shut.

Soon after, Dare heard churns and scrapings of metal on metal, as if a wheel was turning, followed by a series of clangs and clicks pitched in a way that went straight through his brain to make his very bones tremble.

From their center, both doors swung open with an agonizing slowness, as if to prolong every new prisoner's dread. The gray-eyed man revealed himself to be a scraggly servant of undetermined age with a bird's nest of gray hair that looked propped like a crown on the top of his head.

All Dare could see at the moment were shadows behind him, and what sounded like hisses or whispers. The man stepped back, revealing a limp. He wore the dull, brown clothing of a lackey, not a guard, and did nothing but sneer as the guards pushed and pulled Dare through the entrance.

If possible, the inside of the dungeon was colder than the outside. At least it was dryer, but not by much. As Dare's eyes adjusted to the dimness of the foyer, he saw and heard rain dripping through invisible cracks in the roof in the corners. Some tiny streams of water trickled down the sides of dark walls where sconces of oil lights made brown circles of light.

The floor was rough stone, and he saw two puddles reflecting darkly several feet away. The musty odor of mold permeated the air.

He clenched his teeth hard to try to stop his body's shudders.

"To the dungeon-master's keep," the old servant muttered. He coughed once and spat upon the floor.

Three of the guardsmen vanished down passageways and into the shadows. But two, including Hoop, stayed with him. Hoop tugged Dare's chain and led him forward.

They were all drenched, head to toe, but Dare did not have their thick coats. He had forgotten his waistcoat and wore only white shirt, trousers, and heavy boots. Through his wet sleeves that stuck to him, he could see the light brown of his skin beneath. His mud-spattered boots, the leather stained, left clumps of mud where he walked. His toes were cold but still dry.

The guards led him to the far end of the room and a narrow passage that curved, ending in shallow steps that descended a short way to an arched, oak door. The door was made of slats of the fine oak, and had a fancy brass handle with curlicue metalwork that matched the door's fancy hinges.

Hoop knocked.

A perturbed, muted voice called from within. "It's open."

Hoop worked the latch and the door swung gently on its shining hinges.

Beyond the door, a cozy, warm room greeted them. It had high windows covered in white silks, a giant, blazing hearth, and along all the walls shelves and shelves lined with scrolls and papers and books.

The floor had many rugs, so many that the stone floor could not be seen. In the center of it all sat a giant oak desk piled with papers, quills, musty old volumes opened on top of each other, two candelabras shaped like hands holding five candles each, and a pitcher and goblet.

At the desk, bent over a crinkled page, quill in hand, the dungeon-master wrote.

Hoop cleared his throat.

The dungeon-master did not look up. He spoke as if bored. "That will be all. Leave the prisoner here."

"Unguarded, my lord?"

"He is in a dungeon. There are guards everywhere. He is not unguarded."

"As you say, my lord." Hoop turned. The two guards left.

Dare stood, still dripping, in the middle of the room facing the huge, magnificent desk.

The dungeon-master's head was bowed, his body hidden behind the massive desk, so Dare could not see much of him. But he did note the fall of brown hair, red-streaked in the firelight, and realized he was one of the line up of titled men who stood off to the left of the king's throne when Dare had been brought for sentencing just after he'd recovered from his fever. If he was remembering correctly, the man he'd seen was about forty years of age, with a tall build and a short, salt and pepper beard.

Though the room was warm, Dare pressed his lips tight to keep his teeth from chattering.

He waited and waited. Suppressed a cough. Refused to fidget. His chain hung down the center of his body straight to the floor. His collar chafed a little on the left. Once in awhile, as he breathed, the chain jingled.

After what seemed like an hour—but was probably less—the man at the desk glanced up. He pushed back his hair and stood.

His features were not unpleasant, and Dare had remembered him correctly from the throne room. But he would never have guessed this man was the dungeon-master. He did not look at all the type. His eyes were big, almost sad-looking, and full of the room's candlelight. He was well-groomed, his hair silken-looking, his attire clean, expensive, the white of his shirt very white, the braid on the low-necked tunic over the shirt, shiny and ornate. He wore several rings and a cabochon ruby at his throat where the shirt parted enough to show it.

Slowly, the man came around the desk, sad eyes on Dare, intent and glistening.

"So you are Prince Darius."

Dare swallowed. "Yes, my lord."

"My name is Stix, and I am the master here."

Stix walked closer to Darius, hands behind his back. He stood almost as tall as Malory, and only an inch or so taller than Dare. He circled Dare, who held his breath as he did so, then came back in front to face him.

"I see they decorated you in the finest gold." Stix made a gesture toward Dare's collar.

"Fitting for royalty," Stix continued, "but here you are ranked based on your demeanor and the severity of your—crime. You are not a violent person, are you?"

"No, my lord." Dare hated how shaken his voice sounded.

"I prefer all my children to call me Lord Stix."

"Yes, Lord Stix."

The dungeon-master let a small smile curl his upper lip, but his eyes stayed sad. Maybe it was the shape of them that gave the impression of sorrow, but then there was the man's soft tone, and the way he kept his hands behind his back in a non-threatening stance.

"Allow me to apologize for the situation we find ourselves in. Necessary evils abound. My position is in no way meant to dishonor you. It is simply what I do. I watch over this whole place, see that things run smoothly with what tools are at my disposal. Some things are unpleasant because some situations are unpleasant. For example, you are not here for pleasure. This is not a resort. You are here for purposes of punishment, and so the cells are rudimentary, not designed for the luxuries princes such as yourself may be used to. No cushions, no hearths, no wine or pretty servants—of whatever gender you prefer—to fuck. Nothing to do here but think on your crime, to ponder it, to let it sink in and drive you mad or set your mind free, your choice."

The speech confused Dare. Not the words themselves, but the fact that the dungeon-master—Stix—was even bothering to give it. Everyone knew what a dungeon was.

"Many wisdoms have been learned in a dungeon, did you know that? Some of the wisest men have spent twenty or more years in one and been freed to go on and make fortunes and own grand households, or rule towns, kingships or countries in benevolent and careful ways. Have you heard the name Markenisi?"

"No, my lord Stix."

"No? Do they not teach princes in Brookfall of the most famous and notorious rulers of history?"

"We learned the history of Brookfall only." Dare's voice wavered.

"How narrow-viewed you must be. The story of Markenisi is that he spent much of his young life gambling and carousing, raping women, fighting men. He had a young son and wife at home whom he ignored, thinking highly of himself, that he deserved all he wanted if no one got in his way, that he should have for the taking whatever he desired. He went into such debt that the king's guard was ordered to take his house to pay his creditors. When they showed up, he challenged them all, single-handed, to duels. They refused, of

140

course. They surrounded his home. Markenisi saw no way out. He was to be imprisoned, and his game was up. He took his wife and young son hostage, threatening to kill them unless the guard brought him two horses, one packed with food for travel, the other to ride. He would escape, he thought, into another life and continue his debauchery. Of course the king's guard, under orders, could never acquiesce to the demands of a criminal. So Markenisi slit the throats of his wife and child in front of them, then fell to his knees as he was taken into custody. What do you think of a man like that?"

"It is a frightening and tragic story," Dare replied.

"Yes. But you see, while he lived locked away in dark and dank surroundings with time to replay his crimes over and over, with time to learn that life is about more than wine, infidelity, fraud and thievery, more than control over those he was supposed to protect, his wife and son whom he murdered in cold ferocity, he came to a clarity of mind, a light from within, if you will. It is said he became the gentlest of souls, tamed birds and mice, gave his bread away to those who were sick or suffering in nearby cells, and it was as if he opened a door into the heart itself and saw all the reasons why humans do the things they do, the entire play of cruelty and goodness, why people feel the way they do and want what they want, how hurt they are, how scarred and damaged, and how they only want to be free of that. He wrote thousands of pages of journals while in the dungeon keep. He became famous for them. When he finally finished serving his punishment, he became the lord-elect of the town he was born in. The people loved him. He took another wife, had many children, and ruled a prosperous paradise, a rich and wealthy man until his death at a very old age."

Dare said, "That story is real?"

"As real as you are the Prince Darius of Brookfall."

Dare jerked at the statement. His chain pinged against the rug.

Stix took little notice, and walked to his desk and picked up a thick, heavy book, letting it open at random in his grip. *"You cannot change the sky, or the way the snow falls when the wind forms curls of itself upon the land, but you can choose which way to travel, whether it be over rock and bone leaving trails of waste in your wake, or upward, toward the beauty only you yourself can create."*

Dare said nothing.

"That is only one part of thousands of pages he wrote. Here is another. *There is no truth without some falsehood; for every best interest you will find a prejudice to follow for how can we achieve the things we want without turning the phrase to convince the world we are worthy?"*

It was hard to concentrate, as cold as Dare was. And he was worried about Malory, how he was taking this, if he'd re-injured his ankle.

"What do you think of what I just read to you?" Stix asked.

"The journals sound quite interesting." Dare's speech came out rattled, hesitant.

"Of course they are." The eyebrows narrowed and if possible they made Stix's face look even sadder. "They are new to you. All of this is. But you can learn. You are a prince and you are strong. I have a feeling you will be among the best and the brightest."

Dare frowned. "You mean of all the prisoners here? But I have committed no crime."

Stix nodded as though he knew. "Ah, but are any of us innocent?"

Dare had no answer.

Stix put the book down, and then gave a wave of his hand. "Come with me."

Chapter Fifteen

Dare walked carefully across the rugs in his muddy boots. His feet were numb. His body felt clammy and cold, even in the stuffy office of the dungeon-master.

Stix led him to the far end of the room where the bookshelves gave way to an alcove that led to a new passage, and a connected room. The air became colder away from the hearth.

A simple wooden door stood open to the next room. It was fairly well lit with oil lamps affixed to the stone walls every few feet. Dare could hear echoes of the pounding rain within because mostly the room was empty. No hearth. No rugs. No desk.

But it wasn't completely empty. A long, oak table took up nearly the entire length of one end. About fifteen feet away from it was a thick post that reached floor to ceiling. It had a wood beam attached to it crossways from which dangled chains at the ends, each about as thick as the chain hanging from Darius's collar.

Dare saw many objects on the table but only recognized the knives and manacles. Along one wall hung more objects, many unfamiliar, but others he knew well, including leather crops, whips and floggers. Darius had had a collection of such things and used them occasionally on servants, and even a few times on Dare himself when they were very young and Darius did not know what he was doing.

But mostly Darius had fought with Dare using his fists, and never severely hurt him. Dare thought it was because, in truth, Darius could not stand being alone and he needed Dare with him night and day and not off healing somewhere in a sickbed.

Stix moved silently across the threshold. Dare froze. He could not make himself walk one more step. His whole body began to shake.

Stix turned, his sad eyes almost pleading. "Please come in."

Dare shook his head. He had lost his voice again, his throat tight, aching.

"If I have to call the guard, things will not go smoothly, and I have already told you I run this place well, and like everything in its place, on track. Easy. Either way, you will come into this room, Prince Darius. So, shall we do this the easy route?"

Dare stumbled forward, vision blurred.

Stix shut the door gently behind them both and went straight to the post in the middle of the room, where now Dare could see through the filter of his tears metal loops bored into the front and sides at varying levels.

Still standing by the door, shaking, Dare wrapped his still wet arms tightly about his chest.

Stix adjusted something on the post. When he finished, he faced Dare. The sconce-light bounced off his hair and did a jig on the stone floor, ceiling, and walls. His voice echoed in the chamber softly.

"Sometimes I have an overwhelming feeling that I need to apologize for this room. But its necessity is so great that it would be as if I were apologizing for the leaves coming down in the fall, or the end of a year. These things happen so that new life has space and ability to begin anew. It's not a hardship when one looks at every event as a strengthening tool, and change as a gift of all possibility. The opportunity in that is astounding. You stand before all possibility."

Dare's breaths came in low gasps.

Stix walked slowly toward the long table. As if making a casual aside to his speech, he said, "Now, please take off your boots, trousers and shirt and place them by the door for the servants to take."

"W-what?" Dare croaked.

"Your clothes. Please remove them. All of them. They are soaked through anyway. When you are done, please approach the wooden post and stand facing it."

When Dare stood unmoving, Stix said, nonchalantly, "If I call the guards it won't go smoothly at all. Our privacy will be interfered with as well as the depth of this proceeding, and they may treat you roughly."

Dare thought, *Roughly? You're concerned about roughly when you are about to torture me?*

Stix sighed. "You really do not want me to call them, do you?"

Dare shook his head and started to un-do the ties on his shirt.

Stix turned his back and went to the table, head down as if assessing all his tools, his palm trailing the edge as he walked all the way around it.

Dare shivered even more uncontrollably as he dropped his shirt to the floor. One of the sconces hissed as if hitting a bubble in the oil. The brown light of the room was not inviting or warm, but tainted, taunting, indifferent. And the cold. It was so cold.

Dare sat to unlace his boots. Lastly, he unlaced his trousers.

Stix was still not looking at him, but now scanning all his horrible dungeon implements that hung on the wall. As Dare watched him through a haze of shock, Stix caressed one or two of the leather floggers.

Standing, Dare unfastened his boots and set them aside, then pushed his last garment over his hips and let it pool at his ankles. He stepped out of the trouser legs, arms wrapped tightly about his ribs, trying to still his shaking and gather what little bit of body warmth he could.

Without turning, Stix said, "Approach the post and face it, please."

"Am I to be punished for my father's crimes?"

"I am afraid so, and please know that I do not think this is fair but it is the way. I feel as badly as you do about this, rest assured. All my children have faced much unfairness in their lives and my empathy knows no bounds. This is a job I take on with my whole heart open. Because to hide from pain and darkness only allows it to fester. This is a job I care very deeply for. And everything about this place I do with sadness and despair because I can see the redemption yet to be, the whole picture, not just the moment. And it's all worth it, the tears and the suffering, for in the end, you and I will be better for it. We will know purity of the soul and we will revel. We will have a special relationship, you and I. You'll see."

I think not. Despite the gentleness of Stix's tone, Dare was getting tired of him talking. He was very long-winded.

Dare could barely feel his feet. The floor was so cold it burned the soles of his feet, which nearly tripped him up as he moved forward. But mostly he was numb. In shock. And still wet from the storm.

When he walked up to the post, chain dragging behind him, he could see through his tears that little dark dots stained it. Blood. He was sure. His eyes were the only place on his body left that felt hot, fevered. But the tears froze on the edges of his lids from the cold air, and he could only focus on one thing. Standing. Not collapsing. Although maybe if he fell and did not get up Stix would go easier.

But then he thought, *No, he'll just call the guards to lift me and apologize and complain about it again.*

The fact that he could have such a clarity of thought within this nightmare, this foreboding of what was done in this room—what would be done to him—baffled him.

He could not stop staring at the bloodstains. Naked and exposed, he clutched his arms around himself tighter, the chain from his collar pressing cold against his chest.

He waited, shifting on his nearly-numb feet, back and forth on the stone floor to relieve the burn in them. It was no use.

Finally, he heard footsteps approach from behind. He did not turn, did not want to see this man or the tool he'd chosen.

When Darius had flogged him, he'd screamed so loud that Darius would throw the tool across the room, then tackle him and yell in his ear, "Don't do that. Don't scream. Shut up."

Darius did not like loud sounds. Really, though, Darius did not like anything. So Dare had not ever been really flogged or whipped, not by a man, and not by a real dungeon-master. Still, the flogging from those few times had been enough to leave scars.

Stix's voice came up close behind him. "You have scars. You have been punished before."

"Long ago." Dare struggled to speak.

"Then you have some understanding of the process."

"Not really."

"Then I will explain. The temperature in this room is part of the process. It remains cold even on hot summer days. Though sometimes that is a great reprieve for men who have been sweating in their chains. But the process remains. You endure. It is not about breaking you, so much as opening you up. Those who do not understand this fact are the truly uncivilized, those whose minds more resemble beasts. You may not see this now, but you will come to see."

Dare wondered what the most evil of criminals thought of Stix's speeches. If they were uncontrollable, the guards would be there, of course, to make things go *smoothly*. Did Stix say these words to every prisoner? Did he have memorized lectures he gave to particular men depending upon their circumstances?

He thought of Malory again. All his thoughts lately were of Malory. The man would not leave his mind. Dare thought he could take anything for the sake of Malory. That it would be okay, even this punishment, if it was to make sure Malory remained in good graces with respect to the king.

He did not want Malory to worry, but he knew he would. Just thinking of Malory made him feel a little more in control. He could "endure it" as Stix said, for higher purposes.

But now it seemed he was no longer preventing a war, as he had hoped, but had changed into a victim, a prisoner of war.

Stix put the flogger he had chosen onto the floor on front of Dare. "Look. This is nothing compared to what I could have chosen for you."

Why make him look if not to intimidate and frighten him more? Dare stared at the flogger. It had nine leashes, or tails as they were called, each tipped with a bright spot of silver metal. That did not look like nothing. It looked painful. Horrible.

Stix came up alongside him and touched him gently on the upper arm. "Give me your arm."

Dare stretched his arm out and Stix efficiently used the chain and hook to lock his arm into place on the cross bar. Stix walked around behind him and took his other arm, repeating the process.

Dare felt even more exposed, arms up, naked, buttocks clenched and balls constricted in cold and terror. He blinked away the tears.

No more, he thought. *I won't cry more.*

But he couldn't help himself. His leaking eyes. The only thing warm about him were his tears.

Stix put a hand in Dare's hair, combing it back, and ran warm fingers over one shoulder and down his back, petting him, stilling him. "Shh. Shh. Do not fear this. You will be fine. You will be just fine."

The touch did not soothe but felt almost as painful as the cold surrounding him. The fact that Stix's voice was gentle made it worse. He almost would have rather had a dungeon-master who did not try to placate him but only hurt. It might be over faster. And he would not have to think.

Stix made him think. That was bad. Thinking. Right now all he wanted to do was retreat, lose himself into his mind.

"You are quite beautiful, my little enemy prince. You will take this well. Your body aesthetically pleasing, your mind numb with cold, your pretty flowing tears. It is a process of letting things go to gain more, your perspective cleansed and shining will be the reward. But I am sorry it is through this door that you walked. I truly am."

Stop apologizing! But Dare said nothing.

The tails of the flogger were long, at least as long as Dare's legs. Stix picked it up, slowly, and let the ribbons of leather brush by Dare's hip, making him flinch. He didn't mean to, but his arms yanked hard at the chains which rattled in tremulous tones.

Of course he knew he could not get away. But the impulse could not be controlled. His fingers were numb, but he felt the damp scrape against his wrists, as if someone were cutting off his hands.

"You are tense."

No kidding!

"Lean forward and, if you must, you may rest your head against the post," came Stix's too-tender tone.

Dare tried but could not make himself move much. To be stripped bare and chained in a cold, stone room—he'd anticipated such a fate when he was caught, but not after meeting Malory. Not after that.

The prince. He tried to picture him in his mind. His head dropped and he heard it before he felt it. The little clinks of the steel tips rocking together, the whoosh of air as they were raised, tinkling, and the rush of a captured wind snapping against a banner as the tails hit him, *snick snick snick.*

He'd been stung by a bee once. It was like fire against his skin, going deep. This was like that only ten times worse and all over his back.

He tasted metallic salts in his mouth from that pain, though he had not bitten himself. It was as if he'd been sprayed with venomous needles.

He stiffened as he waited for the next blow. It came harder. He cried out. Jerked forward. His forehead touched the post and he kept it there for support.

He had thought he was numb from the cold. But he could feel this. As if cold had taken a new name and form, allowing its icicles to become splintery fangs, forcing an embedding of itself deep into skin and bone.

His mind went up into wintry white heights on the third strike.

He could not decide if the pain was hot or cold. A sting or a throb. Agonizing torment or beyond miserable despair. All he knew was if he had the power in that moment to obliterate life, the world, and everything, he would.

He could not keep even Malory's beauty in his mind. If he tried to focus on the prince, all he envisioned broke into a thousand pieces and scattered inside him leaving blisters of pain.

He felt the fifth strike like a great sword slicing him in half. His muscles bunched up and screamed. He heard them. Full-throated and echoing.

His lungs could not hold air. He gasped and gasped. The weeping behind his eyes burst down his cheeks, a solid liquid sheet.

Whip strokes six and seven were lost to him. He wasn't sure the added pain on top of pain had any evolution. It didn't matter. He couldn't hold himself up now. His wrists felt almost cut through with his weight as he dangled. The metal beads had cut him deep; he could feel the blood dripping down the backs of his thighs.

Stroke eight sent his forehead hard against the post—he must've pulled back a little—bruising it.

He could not think of more strokes of the whip.

But they came. Nine. And ten. Sending him spinning, screaming for air. For anything but this.

For a long time he hung by his wrists. His knees did not work anymore. His toes dragged the stone, feeling broken.

From faraway came a voice. Dare did not hear what it said at first, but then he slowly made out words that sounded like: "You did well; and you did not do well. Each statement is true. Your body goes one way, your mind goes another."

None of what Stix said made sense, the words rolling over him.

"You have yet to find the separate peace within each path you take."

Chapter Sixteen

Dare was still trying to breathe without sobbing; his body felt like cold liquid all over, tears, blood, clammy cold sweat.

He sensed Stix unfastening the chains from his wrists. One arm fell to his side and he could feel nothing in it but the ache in his shoulder. The second arm was the same. Numb.

When nothing was left to hold his balance, he started to collapse, but Stix's arms came around him. He felt heavy leather against his naked back. A unique and strange sensation he could not place.

But then he felt the arms tighten and lift. Stix had picked him up. Dare was not large, but he was not small, either. Stix hefted him easily, stronger than he looked, and that was when Dare realized the leather he felt was an apron that covered Stix's elegant clothing neck to toe.

He doesn't want to get blood on him, Dare thought.

His pain was all over his body in open agony, so while the brushing of the leather against his wounds did not register as more pain neither did it soothe.

As Stix carried him from the room, he kept up his usual infernal dialog in such a benevolent voice that Dare thought he was going crazy. He wanted to run at the same time he wanted to grab Stix and hold onto him, begging for his life.

"All right. Deep breaths. You have come through this part of your journey for now as all must, each on their way in life. You may feel your journey is more difficult than most, and that is a burden for many to face. You may think it is unfair, unjust, that you are deserving of more or less or one thing or another, but true journeys of the soul are not about what is fair or just or deserved. They are about seeing. About knowing. About the self. And the self is so weighed down by seeing only the surfaces of things, what is black or white, right or wrong, good or bad. All are fictions. The true self falls into no one category, no one side. It is all one without barriers, consuming and consumed—"

Dare stopped listening when they got to the big room where a wool blanket lay on the rug by the roaring hearth and Stix placed him gently onto it. Someone had been in that room while Dare was being tortured. Things he had not seen before had been placed on the floor before the hearth. A jug of water and a chalice. A folded muslin robe. Washing cloths and a basin of water. Little glass jars holding oils or, perhaps, medicines.

Stix kept talking his nonsense as Dare knelt forward on the blanket, face toward the hearth. The heat that hit him, wafting upon his face and chest, felt so good he despaired, for he knew it would be taken away from him again and again, and he was sure he could not bear it.

He stole a glance at Stix, who knelt beside him, his leather apron folding in the middle, and noticed that the dungeon-master's face was wet. Tear tracks glistened on smooth cheeks.

For a moment he thought he hallucinated. A dungeon-master who cried for his subjects? Impossible. But he heard the dampness in the voice. The sad tremble of it beneath the words.

"I pity all my children here," Stix was saying as he took up a cloth and dampened it.

The water against Dare's back washed away the blood but not the terrible sting. And it was cold, so cold that he could not help but push himself closer to the fire, shuddering so hard he thought he'd break.

Stix said, "Easy, easy." He patted Dare's damp hair away from his face, sliding the wet cloth over his forehead, his tear-stained cheeks, and then blotting his hair. Slowly, he

153

washed Dare all over, and the wool beneath him caught any stray drops of sweat or blood and absorbed it.

Dare grew gradually warmer. Stix used something thick and cool on his cuts and it finally took away some of the pain.

When his thoughts cleared a little, he thought about how he had imagined this day might come. He had dreamed of dark and evil hooded punishers. Of tortures like whips, fire and spikes, and men screaming all around him. He had never imagined a tear-stained dungeon-master with sad eyes, or that such a man might hurt him and then tend to his wounds by a roaring fire. It almost made things worse, because he did not know what to expect next.

"Why?" Dare heard himself saying, over and over. "Why?"

"Listen with more than your ears," came the response.

"No. I understand you think this is some kind of initiation. Hurting me." Dare's voice rasped. "I'm asking why do you pity your subjects if they deserve to be here?" He jerked forward as a particularly deep wound was probed. How hard had Stix hit him?

"Pity should be, you may think, for those who cannot help themselves. Many of my children have made wrong decisions. Some might have lacked any capacity to view alternatives, and others may have seen better alternatives but gone ahead with the criminal action. But all decisions are centered in gain and comfort, and a fear of never having that, or losing what you already have. Men in fear become savage. And the savage man only takes and destroys, but they themselves suffer as well."

Dare thought of Darius, how even on his darkest days he felt empathy for the suffering of the spoiled, bullying prince. A part of him began to understand. But he was still too muddled to make much sense of it.

He said the only words that came to mind. "I'm not a bad person."

"I would ask you, Prince Darius, what fear has set you on this path? How did you come to be here? What are you hiding? Even if you think yourself innocent, you will find answers to these questions. They may or may not surprise you."

He wanted to tell Stix to shut up. But the man's hands were warm and gentle, and the fire—he did not want to ever leave that fire.

It was hard to believe that an hour or so ago, Dare sat in Malory's warm chamber, in a soft bed, and for the first time in his life he was experiencing feelings of love, exploring new aspects of that, kissing the prince of Shastan like a lover. With Malory he'd felt safe. Trusting and trusted. Only an hour ago.

Now Malory would be livid. Risking himself and his health, no doubt, to meet with his father, to demand—what? If he told the king the truth, that they'd been seeing each other, or worse, that Dare was not the real prince, Malory would be seen as the disobedient son and possibly punished as well. Or worse, the king might see him as a traitor. Malory would have to be smart to avoid his own downfall, but Dare had no misgivings about that. Malory was quick, thoughtful, and conniving enough.

Dare still had hope for rescue, but how long would it take?

Dare turned to Stix, who still showed the sheen of ridiculous tear-tracks on his face.

"When is my trial?"

"What trial?"

"The guards said I was to be brought here to await my trial before the king."

Stix had the audacity to look even sadder. "I have not heard about a trial. The king has made his pronouncement and sentenced you here to the dungeon forever."

Dare's breath hitched. "Is there truly war between Brookfall and Shastan?"

"That is what I hear, my young prince. I am sorry for it, and it seems you are, too."

"I never wanted war. I don't understand how it has come to this. How the king of Brookfall has thrown me away. If, truly, he has."

"You think he has not? You think the king and all his guard have fabricated a ruse simply to trick you? You are not at the center of this. No one cares about you except as an item to bargain with."

Dare felt a little of his old strength return as anger at that simple statement stiffened his sore muscles. "I am not an item. I am a prince."

He heard Malory in his mind. *You are Prince Darius. Say it.*

"I am afraid you may be a prince last now, a prisoner first. Change can tip things over, turn them upside-down."

"So you've said," Dare stated through gritted teeth.

"There now. The pain will recede, but you will be uncomfortable for a long while. This is a dungeon and your room will be stone. Not a prince's chamber, not a luxurious abode by any stretch. It is the way."

He gently patted a damp cloth to Dare's now treated back and hip wounds. Dare flinched. Then, Stix reached around Dare's chest with a wrap—soft, so soft—and wrapped him, tying off the ends of the cloth like a big bandage.

"This will protect the wounds for now. You will have this changed daily by myself or a healer. You may be wondering that I would take time out of my schedule to attend you, but I take an interest in all my children, especially the new ones, and the freshly whipped ones."

Dare's stomach turned. He stared his head toward the yellow flames and tried not to think. Of Malory. Of King Millard. Of this strange dungeon-master who was sad for his "children" but seemed to enjoy his job.

Stix came around to face Dare, sitting up on his knees. He said, "Raise your arms."

Dare looked up and saw that Stix held a rough, muslin tunic in his hands, long enough to drag the floor. "Your attire while here. Please, hold up your hands so I may place the tunic over your arms and head."

Dare did as he was told. The covering was a strange comfort. His nudity had been one more vulnerability, one more punishment to endure. Being naked in front of this well-dressed man whose every command he must now obey had unnerved him.

Next, Stix handed him a chalice of water. "Drink. You need liquids."

The cup was made of fine blue glass, smooth on the curve and carved with grape leaves at the lip. It chafed a little as he drank. The water was ice going down his throat. But he realized he was thirsty. Thirstier than he ever remembered being. Dare drank it down in seconds.

Stix poured him more.

"You may rest here and be warm for half an hour before I call the guards to take you to your cell. Please do not disturb me at my desk. There is an extra blanket and more water. You will be fed later in your cell."

For an unrealistic moment, Dare felt compelled to thank the man. He refrained, and turned his head away.

He rested by the fire, its roar drowning out the beat of the rain, which had not stopped pouring during his entire ordeal with the dungeon-master. He must have fallen asleep, for the next thing he knew, two burly men stood over him in tall black boots, leather pants and vests. Their arms were bare and bulging with muscle. They wore sheathed knives belted to their thighs and biceps.

"Come with us and do not give any trouble," one said gruffly.

Dare blinked blearily. For a moment he forgot where he was. His back ached and stung. Then he remembered.

A voice from the middle of the room said, "He will not give you trouble. I am sure of it. Prince Darius wants things to run smoothly for himself and for us all, do you not, my child?"

Dare nodded and stumbled to his feet, bringing the extra blanket he had wrapped around his shoulders. The long, beige tunic reached the floor. The sleeves went just past his wrists. It wasn't much, but it gave some rudimentary warmth. His feet remained bare. He had not been given back his boots.

One of the guards grabbed the blanket from his shoulders. "You are not allowed this," he said, folding it neatly and placing it on the floor by the pitcher of water.

"I'm sorry, Prince Darius," said Stix. "But blankets like that one are scarce here, and used only for the very sick. We provide a straw-filled mat in each chamber and the robe. It does become chilly here, so we provide loose straw as well as a small tarp for insulation and covering. You will quickly become used to this."

Stix was a man of many words. And far too polite for this place. Dare wanted to ignore him, this man who had beaten him, but a part of himself was grateful for the calmness of him, the explanations. He did not understand how that could be, that he would feel gratitude toward this man, but then he'd lived his whole life with a boy he did not understand, and he'd survived.

The guards pushed him toward the office door. The rug ended and his bare feet hit the cold, stone floor. No longer numb, but tender from the heat of the hearth for the last half hour, they burned.

He bounced a little, and the jiggling made the pain in his back worse.

He was one solid mass of pain, and for no reason. None at all. For he had done nothing but obey his prince's command to take on his identity, and then obey Prince Malory's command to remain in the role and reveal his true self to no one. All he did was obey. Without complaint. Still, he was made to suffer.

It was hard not to feel sorry for himself as he followed the guards down a long, dark and dripping hall.

Chapter Seventeen

The walls made continuous dripping sounds. The guards placed Dare on the upper level of the dungeon. They had descended only one flight of stairs, so he knew he was on one level below the entrance. He had a keyhole near the ceiling at ground level for air and light, but right now it provided only a way for rainwater to get in.

He lay huddled on a rough mat in an inner corner that was the driest place in the cell. The mat was so thin the cold crept through it from the floor as soon as he settled on it. A small tarp with holes covered him. He drew his chilled feet under his robe, but they would not warm.

From where he lay he could see only two more items in the cell: a clay bowl of water and a larger pot to piss in.

Dare's mind swam, trying to make sense of all that had happened. He felt as he had when he'd first been taken right after Darius died in his arms. His back was on fire. The muscles in his shoulders and arms ached. His wrists did not hurt as much, but livid green-blue bruises began to show on them. He only hoped he did not get a fever again.

He'd been displaced twice now in only a few weeks. He tried to recall what Stix had gone on and on about regarding the purification of change. Both times he'd gained a new identity. First he became the hostage Prince Darius, and now he was still an enemy prince in people's minds, in memory, but more importantly to them a prisoner of war. Dare was now a being who had no freedom, no ability to govern his own body, or to say to people like Stix "do not hurt me." People with power and authority could hurt him now at a whim, with full consent from the king.

As he lay shivering in the dank shadows, Dare shut his eyes as exhaustion overtook him. The pain and cold made it difficult to sleep but he was so tired that sleep finally overtook him.

He woke to a guard sliding a tray beneath the bars of his door. It contained a shallow bowl of thin stew and a hunk of brown bread.

Dare did not want to get up. Parts of him had finally gotten warm in his sleep, and the pain had receded, but he knew if he moved, every part of him would suffer again. Finally, hunger and thirst demanded he try to eat. Slowly. As he sat up, places on his back felt like they were splitting open. His shoulders protested.

On hands and knees he approached the tray, taking it up and bringing it back to his mat with the bowl of water. The stew was bland but still surprisingly warm. The dried bread tasted like gravel. He ate every bite.

Everything was darker now. Through the bars of his door, the hall sconces sent a swaying brown light over the floor and walls.

He curled up on his mat again, tucking his feet under him and taking care not to stretch his back too much. Each separate wound pounded like a spot of lightning caught under his skin.

This could not be all there was to his life. This very same day, he had had Malory in his arms. A lover ready to explore. A friend. He wanted that again even if he had to endure days, months or years as a prisoner to prove he was not the enemy the Shastans saw in him.

Outside, the rain continued to pummel the ground and the sides of the dungeon.

For Malory, Dare could endure this. He had to.

*

The dungeon-master himself came to him the next morning, in the cold and damp air, to change Dare's dressing. He looked sad as usual, but his tone was level and caring as he spoke.

"It is a trial by fire of fortitude and strength. To go from princehood to this is a shock, I know."

He knelt and moved Dare's robe off his shoulders so it bunched at his waist. Gently, he untied and peeled away the treated cloth on Dare's back. Dare winced and gasped once as it tugged his open cuts.

"There now, not so bad. Mostly shallow cuts. Hurts more than it looks."

Dare inhaled sharply.

"The tricks of the mind come to test you here. But they are tricks. Men scream and cry and laugh and think they are mad, but it is all tricks. We are not who we think we are, any of us. The mind can hold us back from freedom but once it is open, not even a cage can hold it back. A mere crack in the wall holds wonder and awe."

"When is my trial?" Dare asked, unable to listen to anymore.

"You have asked me this before and I know of no trial. I am sorry, for it seems you were expecting one, and hoping for an outcome that does not include life here in my world."

"Yes."

Malory would be begging his father to hold court over this matter. But how much sway Malory really had over the king, Dare did not know.

In his first meeting with the king, it had gotten him a comfortable room in the palace instead of the stockade and the dungeon. But now, with Malory still injured, the prince of Shastan was not at his full strength both physically and for commanding the attention of a jaded court.

Deeper fears began to build inside Dare as well. What if, now that Malory had time to think about Dare's dangerous and gigantic lie, he'd changed his mind? Hiding a secret that dark and deep risked Malory's entire reputation and kinghood.

Stix said, "The true prison is the mind. Do they have the myth of Lysus and the Underworld of Nil in Brookfall?"

Dare nodded.

"Then you remember that Lysus designed the underground prison of Nil with the errant imperfections of the human mind as his structure. The traps and mazes fall back onto themselves, produce false fronts and confusion, fog, indecision. There is no escape but for the swiftest of decision-makers, or the most creative minds, to surpass hurdles of self-doubt and loathing even when the pits are filled with such dark as to make men question their very worth in existence itself."

Dare thought of Malory again, trying to distract himself from Stix's speech. Malory's fiery presence, those cynical grins. Dare had been on the verge of falling in love. Maybe he already had fallen. And all that had been taken away in seconds.

There was no right in that. No clarity.

"The mind is the greatest prison." Stix pressed cool oils onto Dare's skin. "To come to peace in your mind can take a lifetime. Here you have all time to accomplish this, to accept what you have done and no longer reject the true self yearning to be free from all masks and walls."

Dare looked up and over his shoulder. Did Stix know about him and Malory? It would be impossible.

"Ah," said Stix. "You respond to that. I see you understand me better than you thought you might, yes?"

"To become your true self is the most freeing thing in the world," Dare recited. "Are you?"

"True to myself?" Stix began to preach again. "Why, every day I live here and embrace the truth and the horror that crosses my path. I pick it up and I break it and put it back together to make it see that nothing is as bad what is locked away inside, nothing is more confining than the always impending fear of doom and tragedy and death, and that when we face that, embrace that tragedy, that pain, that suffering of our worst fears that we can ever imagine, only then does fear cease and all suffering cease and the mind is free. The being is changed. The being is now an authentic creation of itself, no masks, no labels, no uniforms or rules. Just purity. And you see further than you've ever seen before. The palette is spectacular, ever splashing with radiant colors fresh for shaping into the true sanctuary and paradise we all seek."

"You see radiant colors down here?" Bitterness set an edge to Dare's voice.

"It is in the mind, Darius. The mind. I speak of uncharted vistas and impossible depths. When you open to all of that, the outside world is but a fleeting scene of the whole, much easier to navigate, to endure or enjoy as the fate wills."

Dare let out a loud breath. "The outside world has cruel rules and unfairness."

"The creative mind finds ways to embrace them or change them."

"In the outside world that exists now," Dare said a little huffily, "has the prince inquired about me?"

"Prince Malory?"

"Yes."

"Why would he?"

"Because we are friends."

"I did not know that." Stix pressed a fresh cloth to Dare's back and gently tied it.

"Your guards did not inform you that I was in his rooms when they broke in and took me and brought me here?"

"They did. But I never jump to conclusions. Why would I assume you were friends with the prince?"

Dare closed his eyes.

"For that matter, why would you assume it?"

Stix brought Dare's robe up over his shoulders, his fingers brushing lightly against his arms. At the touch, Dare's skin prickled and the hairs stood up.

Maybe he had said too much. The king had expressly forbidden Malory to see Dare. But now he figured the secret was out. The guards had barged in, shown little respect for Malory and none for Dare. Why would they keep that secret? Fear of Malory's wrath? Unless they were loyal to Malory, or feeling generous now that Dare was in the dungeon, they had no reason to keep their mouths shut. And Malory's wrath counted for less if they had the king behind them.

Dare figured the fact that they were found *in flagrante delicto* when the guards barged in would further fuel gossip.

Stix put his hands on Dare's shoulders, forcing him back a little. Dare opened his eyes.

"The prince does not rule here anyway. The king does. Not even the queen can come in here without permission from the king. Prince Malory took a tour once of this entire place with his father at his side. He was fourteen. That is the last time I ever saw him down here. He did not like this place. He would not come here of his own volition, even if his father allowed it."

As Stix said those words, a shout sounded through the hall. It was not a prisoner. You could hear guards yelling back at one another all the way to the foyer. Through the small, keyhole window Dare could hear more muffled shouts. The rain had let up. The sounds from outside came through, softened by the dampness and the thick walls.

Stix stood slowly, his stiff clothing rustling, his white shirt flashing at the arm and across the waist where the lamplight fell. He did not look alarmed. His face remained smooth and calm, and when Dare looked up he held his gaze for a long moment.

Footsteps pattered down the hall.

The guards at the door to Dare's cell turned away. Dare heard murmurs but no words. Then silence.

It seemed Stix stared straight into him, as if he could see through all Dare's secrets to his core, unraveling Dare's speeding heart. Locked in with the despair of all that had happened to him, Dare's ragged, servant heart had something light and warm still centered within it, and he was sure Stix could see.

"My lord Stix," said one of the guards, turning back to the cell now. "The prince is at the gate."

Chapter Eighteen

Dare sat cross-legged, very still. The burn from the cuts on his back was fading but still ached. He shivered inside, but wrapped his hands about his knees to keep his body from shaking. His chain fell straight in front of him and the rest of the length was piled in his lap.

He could hear the dripping echoes of the dungeon from far-off, as if every prisoner had heard the guard and stood silent, waiting for what might happen next.

Stix's eyes were almost silver in the dimness, flecked with green as if lit from behind by ghostlight. Without a twitch of muscle, or inflection in his voice, he said, "The prince is not allowed here without the king's order. Send him away."

Dare took in a fast breath.

Stix's head tilted slightly. Their eyes met. Dare was the first to look away, head bowing.

"He's on crutches, sir, but armed. And threatening with some of his royal friends to break down the gate if we don't open it."

"He can try," Stix said.

Still staring at the floor, Dare heard him take a step toward the cell door. Then Stix said, "Send a messenger to the king through the back passage. Now."

"Your message, sir?"

"Ask him if he knows his son is here and if he has permission to enter."

"Yes, sir."

Stix said, "Hmm, I wonder why the prince would choose now to come here with demands to enter. And armed? I cannot fathom it."

But by the dungeon-master's tone, Stix already knew it had to do with Dare.

"Less than a day here and already you cause me trouble," Stix murmured as if to himself.

More shouts came down the hall. The voices in the yard had not stopped.

"Prince Malory orders you to allow him to see the enemy prince," said a guard.

"Tell him the prince of Brookfall is here on the king's command and cannot have visitors right now. On the *king's* command."

"He will not leave, sir. He wants to see you."

A cloak of peace settled over Dare. Malory had come. He pressed his lips hard to keep from smiling. He knew Malory enough, spoiled as the prince of Shastan was, to know he would not stop until he got his way. He only hoped Malory would not hurt himself in the process, or his standing with his father, his realm.

Dare became hyper-aware of everything around him. He opened his eyes and saw in his peripheral vision the glistening walls, the way the light from the hall made them faintly blue-gray with sparkles of white.

Against his knees and buttocks, the coldness seeped through his mat but was lessened now with this new change of events. The freshness of the rain had diffused the dank odor of the cell. Straw lined one side of one wall, and it had a warm smell.

Dare heard boot steps move closer to him again and finally the boots came into his line of vision. He looked up past the neat black trousers, the purple waistcoat embroidered with flowing ivy, the white collar, and into the gray-green eyes. Strands of Stix's dark hair were loose from his braid, shadowing his cheeks.

"We shall see what comes of this."

"He's come for peace," Dare whispered.

"Peace?"

"Between our realms."

"You have no power."

"Oh, but I do. You told me that here I would learn to see, to understand a wider view. I already do."

"You have only just begun."

"I began when I was five." Chin up, Dare narrowed his brows.

One corner of Stix's mouth twitched.

"You think I wasn't listening to you all this time, your sermons, your speeches. But I was. The colors of the world are brighter and always have been for me. And my mind? It's full of dreams and I can see them, all the stories I used to tell myself throughout the years to make it through one more day being bullied, called unworthy, and made less than human. All the days I spent in the prince's chambers locked into a routine I neither chose nor approved. The harshness of palace life despite the velvets and silks. You don't know me. You didn't even ask to know me. You tied me naked to a post and decided to hurt me to teach me what I already know. Pain, subjugation. That my place in the world is not better than another's. You say that you are sorry for it and that the whip is part of the dungeon experience and I must know it for as long as I am here or I cannot be wholly part of it, or whole. But I've already learned that lesson long ago."

Stix tossed his hair back from his face. "Your father taught you all this? Good."

Dare did not answer. Let them think the king of Brookfall neglected and abused him. Certainly, the king had never shown love to the real Prince Darius. They had agreed on nothing. Prince Darius was a disappointment to all.

"How can it ever be good for any person to be kept from feeling secure, or good enough to be loved?" asked Dare, feeling brave.

Stix's eyebrows narrowed in sorrow. "Because no one ever is. And none of us are special in our suffering. We all feel it. One is not greater than the other."

A spray of rain shattered itself upon the keyhole window, letting in a fine mist that shaped itself into a transparent white wing-shape that fell gently to the floor.

"And yet we are all special, too." Dare's voice was quiet. "All beings are princes and princesses in that wide, wide world of the mind you so love."

Stix knelt. His eyes gone dark gray. His smooth cheeks like stone. He put his hand on Dare's head, his fingers sinking into his hair. "You think you know."

"I do know. What is good. And what is not good. If you kill love at its source, if you keep someone from ever feeling it, or finding it, you are helping to create a darkness from which the world can never awake."

"I love all my children."

"Do you?"

"I have told you this. And I am sorry for all their darkness. I don't create it. It is of their own making. But I do teach them to live better within it."

"If you know this. If this is what you teach, then you will let the prince through that gate."

"Why?" His fingers pressed Dare's scalp, tugging at the hair.

"Because the prince is locked out. Because the prince is asking. Because the prince is love."

With a single thrust, Stix yanked Dare's hair up and pushed back with his palm, shoving Dare to the floor on his side. His head and collar met with the hard floor, cracking.

Dare said, as clearly as he'd ever said anything, "Prince Malory has come for peace. And for love. You didn't ask. You didn't see. Has anyone ever put you on your own pole?"

Stix laughed without smiling. "It is not my pole. And it is not my place."

The man might pretend gentleness and apologize for all dungeons everywhere, but he was so like Darius. Something was missing. A thought, an impulse, maybe a heart. But then Dare thought, it might take a lunatic to run an asylum. Or a king.

"Will you let him in?" Dare asked.

Dare sat up slowly, waiting for Stix to push him down again. Lose control. He wondered if losing control happened often for the dungeon-master, but thought not. Stix was so assured, dignified, restrained. Organized. His composure was the sculpture of a lifetime.

"Why should I?"

"Because it would be like letting in the sun." For the first time since the agony of being ripped from Malory's arms, Dare smiled.

Stix leaned back as if he'd been smacked.

He rose from the floor, all grace. Silent. Calm. But not as calm as he might have been hours or a day ago, for Dare could see his hands at his sides, resting gently against his hips. They were fists.

Dare's statement settled on the room with the warmth of an idea starting to form.

Stix walked to the door and murmured something to the guards there. Without turning back, he exited the cell and shut the door of bars. The two guards strode off behind him.

Dare breathed the misted air and thought of the waterfalls back home, and how he loved to gaze at them out the windows of Prince Darius's rooms. Cold as he was, it was still a comfort to picture himself on mossy rocks, grinning, running his hands through the fine spray of the air.

The world was a beautiful place. Malory was at the gate.

*

For a long time Dare heard voices in the yard, and deeper down the halls in both directions. Later, he heard voices of men in the depths of the dungeon, and some in the foyer discussing their current princely dilemma.

171

He sat with his legs folded against his chest, his forehead pressed to his knees.

Whatever Stix had put on his back had a faint scent of lavender. The wounds did not hurt as much now and his eyes were dry and clear.

He did not know how long he sat in the dank and the dim of the cell, for the cloud cover outside kept the light silver and the air misted, but when lunch was brought to him he realized the morning had finally gone.

Malory had not come.

Still, he could feel in the mood of the guards that something was happening.

Lunch consisted of a bowl of thin stew, same as the dinner last night. And another hunk of the same made-from-gravel bread. He forced himself to eat for strength. The food passed easier today into his stomach. His throat was less tense, his muscles more relaxed.

He thought about the falls, and Malory. But more, he wondered about Stix.

If he stayed, he would be put to Stix's tests again and again, perhaps with worse tortures and outcomes, for Stix was like Darius in his sadistic views and actions, and Dare knew that for a condition like that there could be no expectation of change. People were the way they were. Stix and Darius might think they could change others, control them through love or hate, torture or comfort, but they themselves were trapped in a world of no change. Darkness, deception and despair. Even if they got off on it, they were trapped.

Dare sat for a long time, dreaming of the sun.

*

The door to his cell dragged, a metal on stone scraping sound echoing through the hall.

Dare sat up, blinking sleep from his eyes.

Two guards blocked the entryway. They wore the black leather and armbands of many of the dungeon guards. The expressions on their faces were dour.

"Get up," said one.

Dare stood, his muslin tunic brushing across the tops of his feet. He approached and the guards stood aside to let him pass.

They led him through the hall to the front of the dungeon and Dare's heart skipped with hope. This way led out, but they moved down the other shorter hall and ended up at Stix's door.

Dare held back a sob of regret. So soon after his whipping, and not healed, was he to be punished more?

The door opened onto the familiar room with the glowing hearth and big desk. The guards flanked Dare, and all stood before the dungeon-master's desk, waiting. Stix sat behind his desk, head bent, quill in hand.

Stix did it on purpose, making them wait. His way of showing power and control.

Dare wanted to hate him but he looked so serene in his setting of woven rugs and oak furniture, fire blazing, the room next door just aching to be opened to expose all his implements of torture for which he loved to apologize. The existence of this place was Stix's creation. His element. He did not prey on the innocent. Dare could dislike him, even fear him, but hatred did not manifest.

Had he even ever hated Darius? That horrible boy. That mentally disordered prince. Dare *had* cried when Darius had died. He never wanted suffering for anyone.

He wanted to say to Stix right now, out loud: *I am a good man.*

He stood and waited.

Finally Stix spoke without looking up, "Leave."

The guards turned and walked out, the door thumping shut behind them.

Dare watched Stix keep writing, dipping the quill in and out of the ink. Something inside him eased up. He could not be afraid of this man. Darius had taught him more about being himself around adversity than anyone in his life.

Boldly, Dare turned and walked toward the hearth, looking about. On the mantle sat a carved wooden owl he'd failed to notice before. A glass bowl lay next to it, filled with colored bits of glass, some round like marbles, others square or diamond-shaped.

"Did I say you could move?" came Stix's soft voice.

Dare could feel the warmth from the hearth reaching out to renew him. He reached up to touch the rough, wooden owl feathers.

"No."

Warmer now, he walked to the couch, leather-covered, decorated with pristine, dark red velvet pillows. He reached out and picked one up.

"Leave those," came Stix's voice.

Dare could hear that Stix had not gotten up. He did not look to see if Stix watched him, but he could feel the gaze all over his body.

"You are a brave one."

"I'm not brave. Just tired of this collar. And tired of being a prince." He threw the pillow back on the couch and walked to a shelf of books.

"Do not touch those or I will call the guards."

"I've decided you can do your worst to me. I've already been through the worst. If you want to scar my flesh, I care, I do, and I'd rather you didn't, but you're not going to touch me here." He put his palm to the center of his chest.

Dare heard a sound like a chuckle that stopped short. He reached up and took a book, opening it. It was poems. There were hand-written notes in the margins. He saw the words, *A dark ripening begins…*

He closed the book and held it out. "Poetry."

Stix was looking at him now.

"Put it back."

"Call the guards."

Now Stix got up and his boot steps across the carpet made soft thuds as he approached. He reached out and snatched the book from Dare's hand, placing it neatly onto the shelf.

"Strip," he said. They stood eye to eye.

Dare almost flinched, but did not allow his startlement to show. He did not move.

"You are afraid?"asked Stix.

"Of course I am. You're cruel."

"I have been ever so gentle with you. Caring."

"As well as making sure I am placed in the most vulnerable of situations."

"You understand nothing."

Dare stared into those ghost-lit eyes.

"Lose the tunic," Stix demanded again.

Teeth clenched, Dare pushed the material from his shoulders. The robe fell about his lean form and pooled at his feet. The only thing he now wore was the cloth tied about his torso as a bandage for his wounds.

"Satisfied?"

Stix stepped back, no expression on his face, and yet Dare felt the burn of the gaze as it raked him. "You misunderstand."

"I don't think I do," said Dare.

"Follow me."

Every part of Dare's body slumped when he saw that Stix was leading him toward the door to the punishment room. He clasped his hands in front of him, head down, eyes blurring. His loose chain dragged behind him.

Please, you don't have to do this. He wanted to beg. He did not want to beg.

His steps got smaller and smaller. When Stix opened the door, Dare reached out to the frame and gripped it, holding himself back. He held tight, looking at his knuckles as they turned white.

He did not want to look through the shadows, but he'd already glimpsed the room anew and it was imprinted on his vision: the wooden pole with the crossbeam. The curled whips on the wall. The long table with leather and metal objects lying flat, the sharper ones catching glints of light leaking from Stix's office.

He closed his eyes, feeling a warm line against his lashes from the start of tears.

"This way," he heard Stix say from across the room.

He took a deep breath, opened his eyelids and saw that Stix was beyond the table and had opened a door to a side room. Dare had never seen that door when he'd been here yesterday and could now see through it to look upon an orange glowing fire.

Stix stared at him, eyebrows low, but he wasn't frowning. He said, "Darius. Come with me."

The weight on his muscles lifted. His nudity still inhibited him, but only a little. Shadows covered him and he held his arms together in front.

Dare took a step forward, never once looking at the post, and focused only on the new room and Stix, in his infernal patience, waiting for him to catch up.

When he got to the doorway and peered in past Stix, he saw two male servants in rough clothing. They were placing stacks of folded towels on wooden benches. A low table held several flickering candles. Oil lamps on the walls above warmed the room, along with a wood stove. Big pots sat on the stove. Water pots. They were warming there.

A large, metal tub sat between the benches. In it, Dare could see at least half a foot of water. One servant turned to a pot on the stove and picked it up by its handle with quilted mitts. He poured the water into the tub. It steamed as it went in.

Dare saw a hand pump by the stove where they could get more water, and a drain underneath. Everything needed for a bath.

"Into the tub with you," Stix said.

Dare's skin began to itch with just the thought of warm water all over. He had not had a real bath like this in so long.

"Take care not to soak your back. Your wounds are only just beginning to close."

The servants stood to the side, heads down, hands behind their backs.

Dare walked over to the tub. He looked at Stix, then back at the bath.

"Why?"

"You are to see the king. I do not want to offend him with your presentation. You will be seen in a good light, Prince Darius, if I have anything to say about it."

Shocked, Dare could only stand by the tub, naked, unmoving.

"Well?" Stix asked.

Finally, Dare bent and stepped into the tub, the warm water immediately stinging against his icy feet. He lowered himself and could not stop the low moan that escaped his throat.

The water rose to his hips. He bent forward so it would not rush up his lower back. Still, the welts and cuts began to sting. The edges of his bandage became soaked.

His chain jangled in the bottom of the tub, rubbing one thigh. He didn't care. This was bliss. His blood rushed at the encompassing warmth. He felt his cheeks flush. He lowered his hands into the water at his sides and let them float.

Dare looked up as he heard Stix approach the tub and say to the two servants, "I will see to him." He made a hand gesture, like a slice, and the servants quickly left the room.

Stix moved to one of the low benches and sat. He picked up a round, flat disk and held it out to Dare.

"Soap. Use it."

The soap glided smoothly into Dare's hand. When he lowered it into the water and brought it back up and rubbed it into his chest, a white foam appeared. Its lilac scent filled his lungs.

He washed carefully. Completely. Stix sat and handed him cloths, and a small brush for his nails. Dare had not noticed until now that a neatly folded stack of clothing lay on one of the benches. He recognized his white shirt, waistcoat and trousers. They all looked fresh, pressed and clean.

After a long silence, he asked, "When will I see the king?"

"Later."

Dare nodded.

Stix took a pitcher of warm water from the stove and came back to the tub. "Lean forward. We'll do your hair. Let the water run forward off the front so it does not wet your back."

Dare could not believe the dungeon-master was helping him wash his hair. But he did not protest. After the first rinse, he used the soap. Stix poured a second pitcher of water slowly over his head to take away the lather. Dare reached up and wrung the water from his locks.

"Normally you would stand and rinse again," Stix said. "But I am afraid for your back. So I have damp, warm towels to rub you down."

When Dare stood, reluctant to leave the warmth, water ran in sheets from his body. He started to shiver but before he could step out of the tub, Stix wrapped him in towels, one over his shoulders, and one about his mid-section.

Dare stepped out, expecting his bare feet to hit cold floor, but Stix had laid out a towel for him and his feet met only soft cotton.

Stix came up alongside him and took the edges of the towel and rubbed at his arms and chest. He knelt and did the same with Dare's legs. It was an intimate position and gesture, yet Stix gave no indication he noticed.

Having lived with a prince most of his life, Dare knew this was a servant's job. Why Stix had sent the servants away was a mystery to Dare.

He is a sadist, Dare thought, still confused by this man. *But gentle.*

He held out Dare's trousers so he could step into them.

He handed Dare his boots, cleaned of mud and polished to a shine.

He changed Dare's bandage again.

Dare allowed all the ministrations, figuring it was one more apology from this gentle sadist. A question came to him.

"Have any of the prisoners here ever tried to kill you?"

"Yes."

"Not a pleasant job, then, all the time." But truly, Dare knew the man had no problem wielding the whip.

Stix looked up at him with a sad, nearly imperceptible smile.

"Pleasant? Why, I revel in my work. I have much help. And much training. As to threats on my life, the strongest brutes are chained of course, but I can take care of myself. I have loyal guards within earshot as well. Why? Have you thought about it?"

"Killing you? Of course not," Dare said.

Stix helped him into his shirt and waistcoat. He went around Dare to his back and took a comb to his wet hair. Dare braced for the pull on his tangles that never came. Stix was gradual and methodical, taking out the tangles with utmost patience.

"But to answer your question, I find my job quite pleasant. I am providing a necessary service."

Fully dressed now, Dare turned to look at him. "Hurting people."

"Helping people," came the terse response.

Chapter Nineteen

Before leaving the bathing room, Stix held up a package wrapped in brown paper. Dare took it, wondering what it could be. It felt like cloth. More clothes?

He unfolded from the wrapping a forest-green, velvet cloak. He'd seen it in Malory's room during one of his many visits, draped over a high-backed chair.

"This is the prince's cloak. W-why?" Dare held it out, letting the length of it unfold.

"He sent it to you."

Dare put it on, then wiped again at his eyes, which were betraying his emotions far too much these days.

*

The new March grass, frozen from the storm, crunched under Dare's feet in the dungeon courtyard. The iron gates opened before him. Then the larger, more impressive castle gates swung wide, allowing him through.

The path leading to the broad stone steps of the palace had been sprinkled with straw to keep the mud at bay. The flowers on either side had frozen and now glittered like colored broken glass in the sun. On the giant pond the swans hid, nowhere to be seen.

After the musty atmosphere of the dungeon, this air filled Dare's lungs with a sweetness he'd almost forgotten. His body tingled all over. It was wonderful not to be freezing cold.

He wrapped the cloak tighter about him, smelling camphor and Malory.

Guards surrounded Dare as he walked up to the castle entrance. Eight in all.

Stix led the entire party. He wore a regal, gray cloak with the unicorn symbol of Shastan painted on the back in dark blue. His hood was laid back, his long, brown braid of hair reaching almost to his waist.

More guards met them at the tall, double doors.

The interior glowed gold. On tables along the foyer walls, candelabra stood lit and glimmering all around. Sconces lined the ceiling. The marble floor shone, reflecting points of light onto the walls, making everything double-lit. Crystal chandeliers with more candles hung every ten feet down the massive corridor that led to the throne room.

Dare had come here the first day he'd been released from the healer's compound. He had not been dressed as fine. And he had been afraid.

Now he was more nervous than afraid, and anxious to see Malory. It had been only a day since he'd been taken from Malory's arms. His bed. His room. But it felt like a year. He wanted to know for sure that Malory had not hurt himself after falling against the door frame and to the floor. He wanted to see for himself that the prince did not suffer.

He wore the prince's cloak on his shoulders. It was his symbol that Malory would fight for him. It felt good. But Dare also wanted to make sure Malory's temper did not make things worse for the prince. He cared less about himself and what might be decided for his fate than he did for Malory. He wanted Malory to stay strong and go on to become a great king.

Dare had never entertained the notion of being a king. Not even in childhood play. But if he committed to play the part of a prince for the rest of his life, he was now forced to consider it. He needed to embrace it wholly or come clean. He had not yet decided which one it would be on this day.

They all entered the throne room, Stix in the lead.

The color and flash and flare nearly assaulted Dare's eyes which had so quickly grown used to the shadows in the dungeon. Everything sparkled, from hair to faces to gilt-lined costumes. From giant oval lanterns to shining marble unicorn sculptures erupting from the walls. Rings on fingers. Rubies and emeralds on broaches and pendants. Eyes lit with intrigue. Stained glass on high windows depicting benevolent faces, green forests, and unicorns surrounded by stars.

The blue path to the throne—the thick, indigo carpet Dare had stared at intently his first time here—had been laid down for their group.

Dare's heart pumped fast. His back ached. But he kept his chin up and looked straight toward the gray cloak of Stix ahead of him. Beyond, the raised dais appeared with two thrones seating one king, one queen, and their beautiful son, propped on a gold-painted crutch, standing between them.

Malory wore midnight blue trousers, waistcoat and a long, sweeping cloak. The cloak was lined with white fur at the edges of the front and all the way up to the hood, which rested against his neck. His shining, black boots rose to the knee and went up even further in front, as if made to armor the kneecap itself. Dare noted that Malory wore both boots, and that his foot with the injured ankle rested on the floor equally with the other foot as if it gave him no pain. The only indication of his injury was the crutch he barely leaned upon.

Malory's face angled perfectly in the light, showing off his regal beauty. That perfect nose and chin, that bronze skin. Still untamed, his mass of blond hair nearly hid the thin gold crown—more of a band—that he wore.

At the sight of him, Dare felt a sting in his chest. His skin warmed all over. He swallowed tightly, holding the air in his lungs a moment to keep control of himself.

Malory's gaze skipped over Dare, then fixated on Stix. His brows narrowed.

Stix made his way to the line of men to the right of the king. Five in all counting the dungeon-master. The king's men. His inner circle.

The guards flanking Dare stepped off to the side of the blue carpet, four to the right, and four to the left.

Dare saw Stix lift his right hand, palm down, and make a downward gesture. Obeying, Dare knelt on one knee before the thrones, and bowed his head.

He'd been around royalty his whole life, but not like this. His throat was tight. He had to force his hands to relax so they would not make fists.

The huge room went silent. Not even a breath could be heard.

Dare thought everyone there might be able to hear his heart. It pounded. He could not stop the zing of nervousness pulsing through his veins.

Loudly, King Millard cleared his throat. "Your father has not signed the peace agreement between our countries. Further, three hundred troops from Brookfall entered our forests unannounced, in the dark of night. They were dealt with. None lived to confess their mission."

Dare listened, somewhat outraged. If the king still thought his own son was alive, how could he be so negligent? Appalled for Darius, for the betrayal of father to son—no matter that the son had an unstable mind—he also realized with horror that this statement from King Millard would be enough to sentence him to death.

"I would ask you now, before these proceedings go any further, if you have any insight into this madness."

"I do not, Your Highness."

"No insight at all? Not even to the character of your own father?"

Dare took in a shaky breath.

"If I may, You Highness, I can say that my father did not share much with me about why he made the decisions he made. He met with me on occasion to lecture me about my behavior, to tell me what was expected of me, to show much disapproval of me no matter what I did. He is not a man to show love, Your Highness."

"That is unhelpful," said the king. "Is there anything else?"

"With age, he has grown more grim. Perhaps not fit— well, it is not my place to say."

"Are you saying-- would you say your own father is not fit to rule?"

Dare lifted his head, glancing at Millard's face, and then looking down again. "I would not care to dishonor my father."

"But you think it."

Dare did not reply. If he was seen as a traitor to his own people, it would not win any accolades from either side. He could be honest and still lose the game.

"This is not a fair question, Father." The prince spoke up.

"Did I ask your opinion?" The king sounded impatient.

Dare thought, *He's angry at his son. He knows. Well, then, if he knows about me and Malory this could be the end. I will go with dignity.*

But he knew he was fooling himself. Who could be calm in the midst of this? Dignity. What did that word even mean?

"You have been treated well here, have you not?" asked the king.

Dare's back itched. "Yes, Your Highness." Out the corner of his eye, he saw Stix's face harden.

"Dungeon-Master Stix. Report on the prisoner's behavior in the past twenty-four hours."

Stix stepped forward and faced the king from the right of the throne, going down on one knee.

"Your Highness, Prince Darius of Brookfall has been exemplary. He has followed my every rule without protest."

Light blazed from the corners of Dare's vision. So many candles. So much stained glass. The room was ablaze, like being inside a rainbow of effulgence.

"You flogged him well, I should hope, so I can report this back in a message to his father?"

"Yes, Your Highness," answered Stix.

Dare darted a look upward and saw Malory's face go pale.

"Father, you cannot have ordered such a thing! He's a prince!"

"I did not ask for an opinion from you," said King Millard. "If you cannot hold your tongue, I will have you escorted out of this room."

King Millard turned his attention back to Stix. "You have done as I have asked. You are to be commended."

"Yes, Your Highness."

"If he were to remain in your custody, do you foresee any problems?"

"None, Your Highness."

Malory made a soft sound of protest.

The king held up his hand to stop him.

Now the queen spoke. "He is a hostage. The agreement was that if his father did not sign the treaty and broke the peace, his son was forfeit. The king and all of Brookfall should be thankful Prince Darius still lives."

The queen's crown, spiked with sapphires, blinded Dare as he looked up at her. He could not take his eyes off her. She wore a shimmering gown of white and her blond hair, a shade paler than Malory's, spilled around her crown in a hundred, tight curls. Her face was tight and angry, pink at the edges.

"You see, Prince Darius," began King Millard, addressing Dare. "This is an audience I have permitted to discuss your future with us. The dungeon life is one such future for you. If your father has forsaken you, what else can we do with you? We cannot send you back to him, for he has not earned that privilege."

Malory, all blue shadows topped with coppery light as he stood in the direct shine of one chandelier, said, "You never intended to send him home."

"One more outburst from you—" the king warned.

Dare clenched his fingers tighter until the nails hurt his palms. "I do not wish to go home, Your Highness."

"This is the first I am hearing of this."

No one asked me, Dare thought. Aloud, he said, "My father hates me. It is obvious."

"This is a ploy, no doubt," said the queen.

"How is this a ploy? I had no idea I would be taken hostage, Your Highness," Dare said.

"You will speak when you are asked a direct question," the king commanded.

Dare lowered his head. That blue carpet again, finely made but knobby when seen up close. It smelled of soap. Did the servants scrub it like they did the floor?

"Please, Father, may I speak?"

Dare blinked hard. Malory did not know when to quit. "No."

Dare heard the king shuffle his booted feet.

Prince Darius."

Dare raised his head. Beyond the throne, where a high, small window showed the sky, a shadow passed, like a cloud, darkening his vision. It passed in seconds.

"Regarding the matter of my son," the king continued.

Here it comes.

"I am informed that though I forbade my son to see you, he met with you nearly every day that you have been here. Spent time with you. I do not blame you for this. These actions against my ruling were his and you had no choice in the matter."

He couldn't get a breath now.

The king continued, "I have taken the matter up with my son."

Dare saw Malory suck in a hissed breath.

King Millard's gaze flicked to his son, then back to Dare.

"I am informed that you both have created a sort of friendship and I would like to know your feelings on this matter."

Surprised at the statement, Dare opened his mouth and for a moment no words came. All he could think to do was repeat back what he had heard. "My feelings, Your Highness?"

"Yes." The king shook his head once, as if flicking away a fly. "What do you think of the prince? Of my son?"

"I—I think he is intelligent and strong." He stopped.

"Head-strong, perhaps?"

A few chuckles came from the gallery.

"Um, yes, Your Highness? But that also means focused, decisive. He knows what he wants."

"He is spoiled, you say."

"Not as I have seen in some, Your Highness." An image of Darius's unhappy, spiteful face came to him. "He is used to luxury, as any prince would be. But he is no bully. There is a difference between pride of position and arrogance of heart. He is honorable, Your Highness. A good man."

King Millard sat back, eyebrows raised.

Dare saw Stix turn all the way around to look at him.

King Millard said, "You must be aware that my son has spoken up for you, on your behalf. Is that why you praise him to me?"

"No, Your Highness."

Everyone Dare ever met saw duplicity around them. The world did not seem able to exist without it. Including himself. A servant. A nobody. And now here he was.

"Then why?"

"Because he deserves praise, Your Highness." Dare paused, unsure if he should speak further. Finally, "Although he is terrible at backgammon."

More soft murmurs and held-back laughs came from behind Dare.

King Millard leaned forward. His mouth twitched.

Stix stared at Dare as if Dare was crazy.

Malory's lips parted in surprise. His honeyed eyes took on an inner glow and Dare gave him a small smile. The glow increased.

Whatever was to happen, how could things get worse?

"I taught him backgammon myself," the king said.

Without losing a beat, Dare said, "Then I am sure you are an excellent player and that Malory was not paying attention."

More murmurs and laughter came from behind him.

"Well done, Prince Darius. Well done. But the fact that you have put smiles on the faces of some of my most stoic advisors, the matter remains as to what to do with you."

"The dungeon," the queen said. Her face had never shown even a hint of a smile.

Dare said, "Once, not so long ago, an offer was made from Shastan to the kingdom of Brookfall."

"Go on." The king leaned forward.

Dare did not look at Malory for fear the prince would think him a fool.

"Your delegates came to Brookfall and a proposal was made."

"The proposal for a marriage between the two kingdoms for a guarantee of peace," said the king.

"Yes. That proposal."

"Not only did the king of Brookfall decline the proposal, he had our delegates tossed out of the castle in the middle of the night where they were ambushed. The insult was heard loud and clear."

"I never knew they'd been ambushed. And I never had a hand in the decision about the proposal," Dare said. "But if I had, I would have gladly agreed."

"What are you saying?" the king asked.

"I would agree even now."

The king stood now. "You hold no power. No ability to make peace yourself. Now I am the one insulted. Do you think I would stand here and agree to the ludicrous suggestion that a hostage, an enemy of war, would marry my son?"

Dare saw shadows before the light again, coming through the highest window. For a moment, he was dazed. What had he been saying? That he would marry Malory? That he was good enough? Wanted here? He had been the footstool of a prince, nothing more.

He had been one of a group where everyone was slaughtered, and he the sole survivor. He'd almost died of a fever. He'd secretly visited the prince of Shastan every day for weeks after. Then ended up beaten and without hope in a dungeon beset by a storm.

Everything that happened to him in his life had been about what others could get from him. He'd never had a say. Never known free will. Yet he had not complained. He'd seen the world as still beautiful, still worth living in.

But now he realized, as the king spoke of his unworthiness, of his powerlessness, that maybe Darius had been right. That the world was ugly and full of hate. The hearts of humans were all broken.

He swayed. His back stung fresh again. He could not look at Malory for fear of what he might see.

He watched above the king's head as the light seemed to sway and dip and fill the room with odd shadows. Then he saw what it was.

With a voice just above a whisper, he said, "I think—I think the swans are flying."

Chapter Twenty

The court erupted.

Dare shut his eyes against the noise, the world, his fate.

Swans flying. In his own realm, Dare had learned the symbolism meant change, great change, but also revelations of secrets. Even deceptions. He was the deceiver here, the dishonest man. Standing before the king the trying to prevent a war. And the swans were flying.

"Silence!" King Millard stood tall and imposing over the crowd. The tittering voices echoed and receded.

As if from a distance, Dare heard Malory's voice. "Father, please!"

Dare opened his eyes. Everything was a blur. But he could see the dais, the glimmer of the thrones, and the sparkling people upon them.

"The swans are flying?" The king turned and looked up to where Dare had seen them. "This is of great significance to our people. Change is coming."

A low hiss could be heard from the court. A long silence followed. Candles flickered sending streaks across Dare's vision, like a dream.

Maybe it was a dream, all of it.

As if to convince Dare even more that he must be asleep, and that everything happening teetered on the brink of insanity, Malory in his fine, dark blue velvets came around the dais to the lower step, swirled his cloak, threw aside his crutch, and knelt before his father, his golden head bowed.

Dare could see only the backs of his shoulders and the long fall of the cloak where it dragged the marble step behind his stooped form.

"I would beg to you, Father, with my life in your hands. I give it freely if you only allow me to speak."

"Oh, but I know what you're going to say."

"You do not, sir."

Malory's voice held a tone Dare had never heard before.

"I do," said the king. "You are going to ask for whatever you want with no regard to anything but your desire to get what you demand. You are going to say that Prince Darius is royalty and should be treated as such. You are going to plead for him, the enemy. You are going to tell me he is different from the rest of our enemies, that he is a friend, that he has turned to our way of thinking."

Malory did not reply.

"Is this not true?"

"No. It is not."

Dare's body began to shake. He watched Malory raise his head high.

Already, sobs tried to rise in Dare's throat.

"No?" the king asked.

"No."

"Then what is it, my son?"

"Simply this. I love him."

Amidst the gasps and groans and excited whispers around the great hall, Malory's voice rose.

"I love him," he repeated. "And I would be honored to marry him for peace between the realms of Shastan and Brookfall. For now and into the future."

Yes, Dare must be dreaming. For the young and handsome prince of Shastan who could have anyone in the kingdom he wanted, whose very being seemed to leave sparks on the ground everywhere he walked, who would one day be king of all the lands of Shastan, had just declared his love not for Prince Darius, but for the servant once called Footstool from a land of waterfalls and mad kings.

For Malory knew his secret and he *still* said he loved him.

Most definitely, this had to be a dream. Dare had to be asleep on a cold mat in a chamber of stone with a tarp and a cracked piss-pot and only straw to cover the floor.

The throne room was tinged with streaks of candlelight and dark swan shadows.

Dare looked up at the swans that passed over more windows now, winged shapes darkening the stained glass, and waited for everything to fade. For the cruel awakening.

A murmured chant started in his mind. *Don't wake up. Don't wake up.*

The gossiping voices in the crowd behind Dare grew to a loud hum. Dare was dizzy with the sound, blinking again and again as lights danced in his vision. The room had grown hot, the air mixed with the perfumes of the courtiers along with sour scents of perspiration, and the singe of burnt wax.

The dark blue of Malory's cloak swirled.

A pounding began in Dare's forehead. The light turned apple-green around Malory. Then an unsteady dark with stars about the edges. The top of him glowed, a golden orb.

Before he realized it, Dare had lost his balance and fell off his knee, onto his hip and to his side. He put out his hand to push himself upright. His arm trembled a moment, then he pushed himself forward in shock.

Before anyone could speak, Stix strode to his side and helped him balance again.

Malory had turned, and was standing shakily, reaching for his crutch.

Gaze stern but voice soft, Stix said, "Are you in pain?"

Dare's back muscles were tight. There was an itch. An ache. But nothing he could not withstand. "No."

It was not pain that had sent him reeling. But the thought of the dream, and the terrible waking from it. The shock of words.

"It was what Prince Malory said." Dare gasped and looked up. "What he just said."

Malory, the king, the queen and the entire court stood all about, staring at him, eyes wide open, the world firm and alive, not fading and gray.

Dare met the golden syrup of Malory's gaze. His voice burst forth. "Did you just say you love me?"

King Millard's facial muscles tensed and rippled, as if his mouth worked at words he did not know how to speak. Finally, he managed one. "Stand."

Stix helped Dare up.

Malory started down the last step, limping. No one stopped him. He came up along Dare's other side, supporting him at the elbow.

Malory glared at Stix and said, "What the hell did you do to him?"

Stix's gaze remained passive.

"I'm all right," Dare said. "I'm all right." He reached out to Malory's free hand and grasped it, pressing his fingers into his palm, feeling the warmth, the fiery vitality. Could he have him? Would this dream give it?

It seemed perhaps so. For he wasn't waking. But then again, it could turn to a nightmare. The king was looking at them with a fight of fury and confusion in his eyes.

"My father obviously did not want me to marry a Shastan," Dare said. "But in my short time here, I find that I do. I mean this with utmost graciousness and respect."

Dare turned to Malory.

"But only if the prince would want it. Not ever as a forced arrangement against his will."

Malory said to his father, "I do want it. Do you not agree this would be the start of the best path to eventual peace between our realms?"

King Millard said, "If his father disowns him, he does not stand to inherit."

"My father has no other heirs," Dare said. He was clear now, the dizziness gone. "He is too prideful to allow his realm to fall outside the family name. His siblings are all dead. I am his only heir."

"But he gave you up," the king argued. "For all he knows you are now dead at the hands of our executioner."

"I cannot understand why he gave me up. Unless there is some mistake. Unless he himself did not give the word for his troops to cross your border."

Millard put a hand to his chin. "There are none left alive to testify. Our sources of information have dried up. I cannot know what is going on in that court right now."

"I offer myself as a guarantee for peace. I will marry your son. It is all I have to give."

Malory said, "Father, I am in agreement with this plan. It's a good one."

The king said to Dare, "Would you be willing to travel to your homeland and meet with your father?"

A panic began to set in, starting with Dare's heart, which skipped several beats and then felt like it was trying to fold up inside his chest and quit.

Beside him, Malory jerked. "Father, you would put my new husband in peril that lightly?"

"Peril?"

"His father has given him up. It is clear. He might not welcome the prince's return with open arms." Malory's breaths were shallow.

"What do you think your father would do, Prince Darius?" asked the king.

Dare spoke without having time to plan what he would say. "I cannot say any longer. When I left, his behavior was erratic, irrational. He might be sicker now." Could he play this up? "His memory was worsening and he hid it from his court."

Should he ever meet Darius's father again, at least he could maintain this claim the man was sick when he started

194

raving that Dare was not his real son. But then there were the servants who knew him well, so clearly, he could never go back there.

"You do not believe that you can reason with him?"

"No, Your Highness. I do not."

Malory squeezed his hand tightly. Dare's heart started a normal rhythm again, but at a still-quick rate.

Stix still supported him from the other side, hand at his elbow. Dare wanted to pull away from the dungeon-master, forget the sad-eyed man who handled a firm whip.

But he realized as he looked about and saw the courtiers with their curious, jeweled demeanors, and the king and queen on the dais as formal as if this were a real trial, that the three of them created a united front that might be more impressive than Dare, still shaky, unsure, and full of lies, could provide all by himself.

The king asked Dare more questions, which he barely heard. Everything was happening so fast. His mind could not keep up after such a cold night, so little food, and a beating that had broken his body and left him with no hope for a better life.

The king had not yet addressed their confessions of love. As if he had not heard them. Or maybe pending love was not the agenda here. Only the future of two sensitive realms that had been warring off and on for centuries.

Finally, Millard cleared his throat. "I did not come here with any thought to sanction a wedding. And you, my son, have been promised to another."

Malory's hand in Dare's tensed. The air in the entire room changed, as if sensing an approaching storm. The hairs on the back of Dare's neck and arms stood up.

Finally, the king said, almost off-handedly, "But it would be a sound political decision."

Malory let out a puff of air. His body jerked, the crutch tapping once on the carpet.

"W—what?"

Dare saw a succession of images all quite suddenly in a row, as if diverging futures appeared before him. A dungeon cell, himself grown old, thin and huddled within. A gallows, the hemp solid but scratchy about his neck. The king of Brookfall coming at him in a rage, sword drawn, ready to decapitate him and place his head on a spike for all to see. The beautiful, moss-covered castle at Brookfall crumbled to ruins from war. Or, avoiding all of that, he and Malory waving to a crowd from a balcony, hands clasped.

That last image filled him with anxious hope.

King Millard looked at Dare. "You are the one and only heir to Brookfall."

"I am, Your Highness."

"Your illegal visitations to my son are not your doing. And I cannot hold the deeds of a father against his son, or vice versa. I accept that you speak honestly when you say you wish for peace, and that your suggestion that our original plan to unite the kingdoms in marriage of their princes was not meant as insult. Your character has not come into question for your time here.

"I therefore dissolve my son's current betrothal and give my consent for this marriage between our kingdoms."

It was as if the entire room became a giant entity that gave one gasp. Shouts came from the crowd.

Dare had feared a rage from the court, but it didn't come. Instead, he saw smiles. He saw faces plumped in relief. No hate. No rage. No fear.

"Congratulations," said Stix, in Dare's ear, releasing his arm. "But sometimes freedom comes with even more chains."

Dare did not have a chance to respond, for Malory turned abruptly and pulled him into his arms.

"I knew you could do it," he said.

"I don't know what I did," he whispered back. "Except be myself."

"Prince Darius," Malory whispered back. "The real one now."

A lifetime lie, now. And yet, a wrong to make a right.

Dare pulled back, wincing a little as Malory's grip pressed his wounds. But then pain receded instantly as he saw Malory's smile flash into a grin charged with light.

Chapter Twenty-One

"I don't care what they say, the gossip, any of it. You're staying here with me tonight and every night after. I'm not waiting for weeks of wedding preparations and after the final wedding to have you by my side."

Dare followed Malory into the prince's chamber. Their chamber now. His and Malory's.

His life had taken a path from prince to prince. Two castles. Life to almost-death to life again.

Malory said, "I missed you so much even though you were gone for only one night. I came to the dungeon gate. I tried to fight my way in."

"I know," said Dare.

Malory threw down his crutch, turned and took Dare into his arms. "I hope—I hope you feel the same."

"Our last moment together—couldn't you tell?" Dare gave a shy smile.

Malory pulled him tight to his chest. Dare's wounds pulled and he could not help but cry out.

Malory stepped back. "Did I hurt you?"

"The dungeon. It's a place of punishment. There's a process upon entering."

"I heard Lord Stix say you were whipped. But he was supporting you. Standing up for you!"

"He's quite adept at what he does. And careful to apologize afterward and assure me that punishment was nothing personal."

"That sadistic ass. I will have him hanged."

"For doing his job?"

"Let me see your back."

Dare allowed Malory to unclasp the cloak. "Thank you for this, by the way," he said, as Malory pulled it away from his shoulders.

"That is my favorite cloak, and it is now yours." Malory tugged at Dare's waistcoat. "Now let me see your back."

Slowly, Dare disrobed. As he untied the laces of his shirt he said, "Come, sit by the bed so you don't stress your ankle."

They moved toward the blue and deep purple canopied silks.

The excitement of being near Malory, of knowing he would spend his life with him, was nearly overwhelming. Malory exuded an essence of blazing gold, like the sun, and a fervent ardency that Dare had never felt from another. He was a power he wanted to wrap around himself, be possessed by. Where Darius had been weak, insipid, and cruel, Malory was the entire opposite, radiating authority and privilege but the kind that Dare craved, and realized he'd been craving his whole life.

He pushed back his shirt and his body thrummed with exhilaration and delight that Malory wanted to look at him. To touch. To hold. To make love.

But there was a darkness in the prince's eyes when he saw the wide, long bandage wrapped tightly about Dare's chest, the ends tied neatly to keep it in place.

"My father was cruel to order you to the dungeon."

"He doesn't know me."

"He had time, like me, to get to know you. I went round and round with him before you ever came to the throne room today. All morning, we fought. I told him about you and he still treated you like a criminal when you first spoke up today. I will never forgive him."

"He has to put on a mask for the court."

"Perhaps." Malory's fingers traced the line of the bandage up over Dare's shoulder and lightly over the back, placing his palm flat there as if for comfort. "I can feel the heat. Stix whipped you when you are not a criminal and never have been. He may have been doing his job, but I still would like to see him suffer."

"He is doing his job as commanded by the king. I just want to be with you and not think about the rest of it right now, for I feel as if I have been in a dream my whole life."

"And now I am part of that dream…" Malory's voice went low and faded.

Dare put his hand on Malory's chest. "You're the only real thing. I knew it when we first met and you stormed through my sickbed door."

"It seems like only yesterday. And forever."

Dare nodded.

"I didn't know what to make of you. Were you really an enemy? I had to know what my former intended was like." A wry smile. "Especially since my father was going to marry me off to a noble and I was so unhappy about the choice."

"You would have been unhappy with this choice had you ever met the real Darius," said Dare.

"Never say that again. You are the real Darius. And this will be our final conversation about it."

"I filled that role for him for much of my life in public, but now to fill it forever feels strange."

"Think about it being for the greater good." Malory cupped Dare's jaw, thumb stroking his cheek.

"It is such a huge lie."

"Everyone has secrets."

"I can never go home."

"I know. Or at least not for a very very long time." Malory leaned forward and placed a soft kiss on the side of his mouth.

Dare reached up to pull him closer.

*

Dare had not eaten a full, good meal in two days. On their way to Malory's chambers, the prince had ordered a meal brought up. Their precious moment was interrupted by a bang on the door.

Malory's anxious face took on an edge of anger. "Damn, it's the supper I ordered." He called out, "Come in."

Three servants came in carrying large trays and set them on the table.

"Are you hungry?" Malory asked.

For you, Dare wanted to say, but allowed himself only a nod.

It had been a long day, and now the scent of baked fowl and fresh bread and gravy over carrots, potatoes and onions made his mouth water. And there were sweet pastries dribbling with fresh sweet cream.

They ended up at the table, Dare still shirtless, managing only a few bites. Malory ate almost nothing, but poured himself two glasses of wine. Their eyes lit on each other second to second, the light in the room fading but brilliant inside their thoughts.

Dare had only one glass of wine and it went to his head fast, dazzling him. It made him not care about the ache in his back anymore. Everything in him strained for Malory.

Malory watched him as he put his fork down and shifted in the chair.

"You need to eat more."

"The food will be here later if we get hungry."

The prince smiled. He had thrown his beautiful cloak, along with the one he'd given to Dare, over the back of a chair, and the blues and greens of them had twined together, spreading to the floor like a waterfall at dawn.

Malory stood and Dare jumped up, despite his wounds, and helped him to the bed. They both crawled upon it, side by side. The big windows let in views of distant mountains, the sky pinking along the rims.

In the tawny shadows of the flickering oil lights, it was easy to slide into one another's arms. Easy to let their faces press cheek to cheek, jaw to jaw, then glide toward a meeting of lips and open mouths.

Taste of wine. Taste of sweetness. Malory's hands in his hair, weaving, tangling.

Dare held him fast and tight, so tight he could feel both their heartbeats thundering in their chests. Malory's other hand came up his back, soft over the bandage, but still Dare drew a fast breath and let out a pained hum.

Malory drew his lips to his ear. "Sorry. Can you continue?"

"Of course." Dare pushed him onto his back and leaned over him, undoing the ties on his shirt. Everywhere new skin was uncovered, he touched and petted.

When the shirt was off, they embraced again, and kissed for a long time. Dare felt more lost than ever in that kiss, as if the world were made only of clouds and soft wind, his body a thing of joy. He loved the feel of Malory's bare chest against the buds of his nipples, just barely revealed by the edge of the bandage. He pushed his upper weight on top of him, resting his knees to the sides of Malory's hips.

When they were breathless, Dare sat back and to the side. They each took time to rid themselves of their boots and trousers.

Dare looked at Malory's bad ankle and said, "How is it?"

"Not great. But better."

Carefully, Dare lay back on the soft spread, feeling gathered into blue and more blue, dark and sinking, his bare skin prickling in the cool air, slightly trembling. He barely felt the wounds on his back. Arousal trumped that pain, and his body sang with anticipation, taut in drawn need.

Malory came over him this time, and Dare could see him outlined in the waning dusk, strong and lean, shoulders firm, ribs edged with the golden air, waist curving to narrow hips and a stiffly, yearning cock. That satin stiffness nudged Dare's hip and he reached up, almost frantic now, his own cock waving, surging with his every heartbeat.

Their bodies pressed. Hands clutched Dare's shoulders. He wrapped his own arms about Malory's back, touching the sleekness of it, fingers tapping along his spine.

Their hips met, cocks squeezed together, and the rush of touching so intimately nearly undid Dare. He pushed up. Malory slid a little, up and down, creating friction.

The bliss of that almost made Dare angry, for he wanted more and more and nothing else forever. He wanted to take this feeling and this man into him and just run away, become lost in the mists of love with no one but him in his eyes, lungs, heart, and mind.

Malory moved up and leaned back.

Dare said, "Don't leave me," in a surprisingly small, pleading voice, but was only pleased to realize the movement generated only more pleasure as Malory took one of his erect nipples into his mouth.

Dare stretched in ecstasy, a loud moan escaping him. He arched uncontrollably when Malory kissed a path over his bandage and to his exposed abdomen, then kissed the delicate head of his cock.

"Last time," Malory murmured, "I wanted to taste you so bad, only to be interrupted. This time I won't be stopped."

He sucked Dare's cock into his mouth, gentle and slick at first, warm and comforting. Then Dare felt the pressure of his mouth taking him, seeking that inner taste.

Dare's back was still too sore to move much, but he bucked his hips a bit, trying not to lose control. He had never felt anything like it. He'd done it for Darius, this type of pleasuring, but only as a chore. Doing the act had aroused him. But never had he had it done to him, or felt such a surging in his veins, such fire. He wanted more.

Malory sensed this, and moved his mouth up, his tongue laving just the right places until his balls tightened and his cock jerked; he cried out. "Oh, that's so—I'm coming!"

He meant for Malory to pull away, or for himself to pull back, let it happen, but instead he thrust unconsciously. But Malory was there, holding him in place, and kept him in his mouth as he let go.

He felt every spurt like crashing through doors of lightness and being as Malory suckled. It was too much. He thought he would roll and roll forever in this haze of euphoria.

Then Malory was cradling him, careful of his back. And Dare stretched long and still hard between his legs, enfolding him in a hug, and letting himself be enfolded.

He reached between them and took Malory's cock in hand, feeling it surge at his grip.

"I want to taste you."

He'd done this before. But Malory was not a chore. He was pure delight, and Dare fed on his sweet, hard cock until the nectar coated his throat. He heard Malory yell as if from faraway.

The dusk had turned to sparkling night, not black outside yet, but dark and silvery, bright as a reflecting pool. Malory pulled a soft coverlet over them. Dare dozed, face in Malory's neck.

He woke maybe minutes later, and the room flickered in its dim, pale lighting. He breathed Malory in and let that salt and spicy sweetness linger in his lungs and fill his veins with heat again. He lay quite still, reveling in the sensation. All over his skin flushed.

"I feel you wanting me," came a low voice in his ear.

"I never stopped."

Malory leaned over and kissed him. "Do you know how it is between men, I mean if they want to, um,--"

"Yes," Dare interrupted. "I know." Darius used to speak of it— concerning both men and women—using explicit

204

and derisive terms to describe any and every sexual act in all combinations. Dare had grown used to it. But now—

Dare said in a whisper, "I know how men fuck—each other."

Malory chuckled, then stroked Dare's cheek. "Yeah, but it would be different for us, not just that—"

"—Fucking, you mean," Dare supplied.

"Yes, but not just that, but—but—"

"Yes, I will make love with you like that," Dare said, pushing him back, laughing. "Anything. Everything you want. As long as it's just with you."

Amid fits of suppressed laughter, Malory bought out a vial of oil.

Laughter turned to reverent moans. Malory surprised Dare by spreading his own legs, lifting his knees, and offering himself first.

The oil smelled of new leaf and spring rivers.

Dare wanted to go slow. Malory was quicker, hypercharged, hot and demanding. He flashed with arousal, from glittering eyes to shaking thighs.

Dare put the oil on him, gently stroking, hesitantly probing.

"I've done this before," said Malory. "Don't treat me like a virgin."

"You have? With who?"

Malory grinned wide. "Let me put some on you." He reached up and took the vial from Dare, pouring a liberal amount on his palm, and then gripping Dare's cock. He milked it sweetly.

"Ah." Dare's head went back.

"I'm so ready," Malory said.

Dare felt Malory line him up. He pushed as Malory arched forward. "In," he demanded. "In. More. Just *do* it."

"I don't want to—"

Malory thrust up, impaling himself, and Dare let out a surprised cry. It felt so good, so hot. To be joined to another in such an intimate way filled him with awe.

"Oh—" Malory groaned. His eyes rolled back, chin up. He reached for Dare. "Come here." Voice a sound like rain on gravel.

Not thrusting, Dare simply rested his weight against Malory's chest. Malory's arms came up and around them, holding him close. They remained still, everything a watercolor of steel on steel, gray and mist and the blue-blue depths of the bed.

Dare felt the inner muscles of Malory move slightly, clutching, and everything was so smooth, the air, the satins of the coverlets, the skin of his love—inside and out. Their lips met, and in that slick space between them, low and hot, slowly they both began to move, soft undulations at first, fluid and gliding for long minutes. Serene and good. So very very good.

"That's so right," Malory breathed against his cheek, fluttering his hair. "You're doing that just right. It's hitting something inside me—I want to explode."

"It's amazing." Dare laughed, then buried his head at Malory's shoulder, feeling Malory's hand come up and pet the back of his head.

"You can go faster," he said. "Pull out to the tip, then go back in deep. Then do it again, faster. I want it."

Already the words were sending Dare into a frenzy. He felt himself milked by encasing slickness as he obeyed Malory's command. His hips moved back, then forward. He repeated the gesture at Malory's encouragement again, then again. Faster. Until there was nothing but the two of them approaching the purity of awestruck rapture.

Every part of Dare seemed to be coming apart, and he heard Malory calling out his name, "Come into me. Come. Dare!"

The prince's hands were on his hips, moving over them, petting, fingers digging into his buttocks as he thrust forward again, again.

Dare put his hand between them and stroked Malory's stiff, beautiful cock.

Shouting. Heaving. Coming. Both of them at the same time. Dare pulsing in liquid heat, Malory spilling over Dare's fingers and onto his own chest. Precious and glistening. Chest rising and falling. His lover. His love.

"You're mine now," Malory chuckled, still breathing hard.

"My prince," whispered Dare as he collapsed into his beloved's embrace.

A great wind blew against the windows, rattling the panes.

Neither heard it, nor cared.

Epilog

They both wore white. Satin-lined velvet cloaks. White trousers. White shirts. Boots of the palest leather imported from Bry. The only color on the grooms were sapphires sparkling at each of their throats—matching necklaces, a wedding gift from the king—and the thin golden crowns tipped with leaf-points that each prince wore on the top of their heads.

Dare had never been more nervous, nor more happy.

During the ritual of the wedding, the one moment when Dare thought he might break down completely was not during the king's final pronouncement, nor when Malory kissed him in front of the entire court. It was when Malory gave him a ring shaped in the form of a golden unicorn and said, "You're one of us, now."

When Malory put his arm around Dare and turned him to face the crowd, Dare leaned toward him and whispered into his ear.

"I love you."

"And I love you, Dare."

Dear Reader:

Thank you for reading my fantasy romance.

If you enjoyed this, you might also enjoy subscribing to my newsletter. I put it out about six times a year to announce new books and upcoming projects, and I always have sales and freebies to offer readers both from myself and other authors I enjoy reading. If you subscribe at the link below, you can get a free copy of my book "Letters to an Android".

At this writing, I am working on the sequel to this tale, "The Imposter King." It should be available summer of 2018.

Happy Reading!

Wendy Rathbone

Contact links for Wendy:

Facebook: https://www.facebook.com/wendy.rathbone.3

Blog: http://wendyrathbone.blogspot.com/

Newsletter sign up (you get a free copy of the critically acclaimed "Letters to an Android"): https://www.instafreebie.com/free/3ErH0

About Wendy Rathbone

I love to write. I have this thing about words and how they are used to describe beauty, love, and all the things that open us up inside to our true self, our power. Words do that for me. They make me happy. The new moon smiling, the sadness of a fallen feather at dusk, predatory eyes gazing through smoke.

The reason I write romance these days is because the overwhelming power of falling in love (which has been proven to heal even cancer) is a game-changer. It makes sad people instantly happy. It makes bleak reality look sun-warmed and friendly again.

I have written in all genres: scifi, fantasy, horror, paranormal, contemporary, erotica, romance. My poetry has won awards, publishing contracts, and was recently nominated for a Pushcart. I am a hybrid writer, publishing both indie (under my press name Eye Scry Designs) and with publishers, most recently with Dreamspinner Press.

I keep coming back to romance. Gay romance. Male/male romance. Maybe it was the wonderful start I got when I was very young in Star Trek slash fanfiction. Something about that stuck. The idea of two men falling in love in a society that has winced at that sort of thing for far too long (when in ancient times and other cultures it is considered normal) is alluring. The forbidden is imminently appealing and erotic to me. Many of my themes involve abduction, pleasure slavery, indentured servitude, imprisonment. It's like, with my writing, I'm constantly breaking out of some self-imposed cage and letting my wings unfurl until I can finally fly.

This is why I write. This is what makes me burn.

All my books are available on Kindle and Createspace. So if you have the urge, go take a look. See what's on the shelf.

Love to you all!

210

Ganymede: Abducted by the Gods
Wendy Rathbone

My name is Ganymede, and I have been betrayed.

Every boy my age dreams of leaving home to embark on a noble adventure, but never does any boy imagine it happening as it did to me. On the evening of my 18th naming day, when I expected no more than a chalice of wine and a few drunken flirtations to tempt my innocence, I was instead sold by my father to the god, Zeus - not because of anything particular I had ever done or said, but solely because I am considered beautiful among mortals, and my father found more value in a few gold coins than in the well-being of his youngest son.

To be honest, I never believed in the gods, but my lack of belief held no power in Olympus or on Earth. Now under Zeus's influence, I am kept drunk on ambrosia in the sun-lit halls of the immortals, alternately amazed and horrified at the power these beings hold over others, and how darkly they influence the progress of humanity itself. How very much I want to hate Zeus for kidnapping me, and yet he shows me mostly kindness, even on that fateful night when we shared a bed for the first time. Kindness, yes, but also a godly and unyielding refusal to take no for an answer... probably because he could read my ambrosia-fevered curiosity as much as my naive, inexperienced terror. He owns me, after all, just as he owns everything else, so perhaps it never occurred to him that a captive and a slave might not make the best of lovers.

Throughout my time at Olympus - who's to say how long I've been here, for time on Olympus is not the same as that on Earth - the only thing that gives me hope comes to me in dreams and visions. His name is Sable and he is a magnificent shape-shifter in the form of a giant raven. When he first spoke to me in my mind it was with a resonance unlike any I had ever known - his mind and mine sounding a single note together, a song without words, a promise of freedom, a glimpse of some distant but very real possibility of this thing we humans call Love. But now he is silent. Perhaps I dreamed his voice. Perhaps I have finally lost my mind...

www.eyescrypublications.com
Also on Amazon or order from your favorite bookseller.

ZEUS (Conquering His Heart)
WENDY RATHBONE

When I throw the lightning and summon the thunder, it isn't always out of anger, but often from a love so all-consuming it could only be the effect of Eros himself. Yes, he is beautiful. Of course he is. How could he be otherwise, with hair the color of sunlight and white-feathered wings that drape to the floor? And he is as ancient as the myth of time itself, an immortal with powers and glamour beyond my ability to imagine. He struggles to teach me wisdom, control, strategy, yet I sit here babbling like a child, for all I can think of is how I might try - at least let me try! - to prove myself to him in some way that will cause him to crave my company and my touch, just as I crave his.

I do not yet know how to be a god, for I am only 18 and still just a silly boy who has fallen in love with Love himself, while my father Cronus plots and schemes to lock me in his dungeon and make me his slave forever.

A male/male romance.

www.eyescrypublications.com
Also on Amazon or order from your favorite bookseller.

PREY
Wendy Rathbone

When the rescued slaves were first brought on board my ship, I saw only the one. The one they called Arcana. And though I realized the others had all suffered similar fates - fearsome torture and erotic conditioning that had estranged them from whoever they had once been - I focused on the one who met my eyes with what could only be interpreted as a defiantly seductive lure, while the others held their gazes downward, at their feet, at the floor, at the past which had shaped them and undoubtedly doomed them to any sort of normal life.

Not so with Arcana. That one had no shame in whatever had happened to him. In that one blinding moment when we saw one another for the first time, I knew he was as brash as he was beautiful, and I knew without any doubt that he had chosen me - though for what dark agenda, I could not have said.

My heart went cold and silent in my chest. My throat was dry. My breathing faltered and I was forever changed.

***

We danced. Captain Mordecai and I. Not any traditional dance, but a dance of power. A battle of yin and yang, light and dark, pleasure and torment. A dangerous dance of right and wrong in a single moment caught outside the tendrils of Time.

It was easy to see the raw and sensual power in that man's gaze. But also the fear. Fear of being seen for who he was behind his carefully-constructed masks. Fear of finally surrendering to the dangerous desires he clearly felt when he looked at me, knowing my past, knowing I had been enslaved by sadistic aliens. Knowing I had not only enjoyed it, but had come to love my master. All the wrong things. So very wrong.

That was when I knew he wanted me. That was when I knew I needed him.

That was when I knew I had him exactly where we both needed him to be.

www.eyescrypublications.com

Also on Amazon or order from your favorite bookseller.

LETTERS TO AN ANDROID
Wendy Rathbone

Cobalt is a created human, vat grown and born adult, with no human rights and indentured to serve others for the duration of his life. Liyan is a young man with wanderlust in his eyes, embarking on a career that takes him to the furthest regions of space. The two become unlikely friends and create a memorable long-distance correspondence. Through Liyan, Cobalt gets to explore the universe, living vicariously through his friend's wave transmissions. A strong bond develops between them that not even the stars can put asunder.

———————————

Now you know an android who writes poetry.

This is all your fault. Did you not read my last wave telling you extracurricular activities for my kind are discouraged? Of course this is harmless and strangely enjoyable and does not necessarily require me to leave the hotel. Pel would not care if I wrote lines of equations or nonsensical juxtaposed words. As long as the act does not bring my mental state into question.

However, in history, poetry is often written by the rebels.

So we can keep this to ourselves.

Let me know about your lieutenant's test.

And to give you peace of mind, I never believed you observed me as anything other than human.

Some people are and always will be hateful bigots. Most people are simply uncomfortable in speaking to "property." And anyway, friendship, like poetry, is also discouraged.

Your friend,
Cobalt

www.eyescrypublications.com
Also on Amazon or order from your favorite bookseller.

SCOUNDREL
Wendy Rathbone

Antares is a willing sex slave, trained in the harems of Anada since the age of 18, and owned by a wealthy master who spoils his slaves. But all that changes when Empire soldiers invade Antares' world and he is taken away from the only life he's ever known.

In a colonized galaxy where starships are as common as houseflies, and a dark Empire seeks to control thousands of civilized worlds, there are those who fall through the cracks and refuse to be conquered, including the pirate, Slate, and his crew.

Out in the darkness of the unknown, among Empire soldiers and scoundrels, will bad fates befall Antares and his fellow captive companions?

Will Slate finally find the love he's been looking for his whole life?

Can Slate and Antares ever see eye to eye?

A male/male romance to end all male/male romances!

www.eyescrypublications.com
Also on Amazon or
order from your favorite bookseller.

LACE
Wendy Rathbone

Lace is a being from another dimension on Earth. He cannot die and humans call his kind "vampire" and declare war on them.

Firi is a human military soldier, a trained guard, who has met Lace twice in his young life and formed a bond with him.

In a world where humans and vampires are arch enemies, where vampires are eradicated in horrible ways, where being a vampire-lover means a death sentence, can Firi and Lace ever find each other again and explore the feelings they have for each other?

Will Lace be able escape his government prison, and the amnesia that keeps him from accessing his true powers?

Can Firi, the boy he met in the woods ten years ago, ever hope to help him?

A male/male romance about secrets that can get you killed, impossible rescues, and old lovers who cannot be trusted.

www.eyescrypublications.com
Also on Amazon or
order from your favorite bookseller.

The Foundling
by Wendy Rathbone

Diego is a powerful man with a tragic past. Out on the expansive ocean in his private yacht, he discovers a beautiful and mysterious man adrift on a raft, near death. The bond that forms between them in the aftermath of Alec's rescue is one of fierce passion, though lacking in trust. Can they make it work, or will Alec's amnesia bring forth secrets so disturbing as to tear them apart? A passionately erotic love story of desire and darkness, exquisite and explicit.

———————

I can see his struggle between gratitude and uneasiness. He is buffeted by all things new and strange. He does not know where he is from, who he is or what happened to him. He does not know me. There has not been enough time to transition between strangers and friendship.

This isolation of his is something I can identify with, but it is also a feeling no one can help him with until or unless he gets his own life back. And his memory.

If that doesn't happen, then it will take time for him to build a new life. He is polite to me, even friendly, but even a night together during a storm with his arms wrapped tight around my waist doesn't calm the surge I see inside him, the emptiness, the loss, possibly even panic. That night may have reinforced some trust in me, but so far not enough for him to completely relax.

He seeks me out, though. That's something. He sits by me at dinner when he can have any seat of his choosing. I watch him closely when he does not realize it. At dinner the following night after we had only 'slept' together, and before we go to bed again in separate rooms, I notice everything about him, how he moves, the way the air warms when he is closer to me, the dry sheen of his lips as they part for more air when he is reacting to something, or speaking, or eating.

His hands still shake. Anyone else might not notice because he keeps them clasped into fists at his sides or, while sitting, pressed tight to his lap.

I spend another fretful night alone. I dream restlessly, wild, loud and colorful visions I cannot recall at all as soon as my eyes open. All I know is the dreams leave me unfulfilled, impatient.

www.eyescrypublications.com
Also on Amazon or from your favorite bookseller.

SONS OF NEVERLAND
by Della Van Hise

"The virtuosity shown here is only the beginning of a pyrotechnic talent unfolding into the hidden dimensions of the human and nonhuman spirit."
-Jacqueline Lichtenberg

Set against a backdrop of contemporary culture, *Sons of Neverland* explores the universal questions of love, sex and death - the three most crucial challenges every human being must face. Stefan London is a grieving man, suffering through the loss of his young daughter. When he goes to a science fiction convention in the hopes of meeting her friends, he encounters instead a young man who is dangerously seductive and undeniably magical. Lured into the night, Stefan soon discovers himself in a place where vampires are real, and the world is not at all what he has always believed, and immortality is only a deep red kiss away.

But the price of eternal life is high, and as his handsome maker warns, "Through my blood you will learn a secret which will compel you to live forever, yet a secret so sinister it will haunt you for that same eternity."

The secret will haunt you, too.

———

"This book zones on the question of immortality. However, this is not just the decadent historical immortality of the long-lived vampire, it is immortality as a change in one's perception. This is the story behind the story, delivered by characters that are hyper-real - each one loaded with symbolism. *Sons of Neverland* will have you filled, even brimming over with the sense of Mysterium Tremendum et Fascinans. Go there for a full helping of the numinous." (A Reviewer on Amazon)

www.eyescrypublications.com
Also on Amazon or order from your favorite bookseller.

Prince of Umberlight
Alexis Fegan Black

"If Prince of Umberlight doesn't rattle your cage, you're more dead than the undead!" - **Night Readers**

Thorn may be an 800 year old vampire, but he does not possess the ability to create others of his kind, and so he is cursed to fall in love with mortals, only to watch them grow old and die. Torn by grief, Thorn denounces his immortality and enters into a comatose oblivion for decades.

When he awakens, he is no longer in London, but finds himself in a world spun into being by his own desires - a world where Time and Death do not exist, a world where it is forever autumn, where the Parish of Shadows and the River of Stars become his home. It is in this world of Umberlight that he meets Atom - an interloper into his private sanctuary, but also an impudent imp who is destined to reveal to Thorn the three dangerous elements a vampire must possess in order to become a Creator.

The Art of Brutality.
Submission to Dark Desire.
Love.

www.eyescrypublications.com
Also on Amazon or
order from your favorite bookseller.

YEAR OF THE RAM
Della Van Hise

Year of the Ram was described by one reviewer as... "A space-faring male/male romance full of love, angst, and longing."

Only after Star Commander Morgan Diego becomes an exile as a result of a Galaxy Corps political blunder does he begin to realize how much he valued the companionship of his second in command - the mysterious Lucien, an Alfarian who is more elven than human, with peculiar powers & abilities which begin to unfold as he, too, realizes what he has lost.

Separated by circumstance from his former life, Morgan is thrust into a world where he must survive by his wits. When he meets a peculiar little old man calling himself Kim Le, Morgan finds himself in a situation where he is required to master The Art - not only a form of human & extraterrestrial martial arts, but a way of living and being that will alter his life forever.

At the temple, he is introduced to his new teacher, another Alfarian who begins to steal his heart - a heart which is already promised to Lucien. Torn and conflicted, Morgan struggles with the world he left behind and the world he now inhabits.

Beginning to believe he may never again return to his ship and to the friends and loved ones he left behind, he is all the more frustrated and heartbroken when a new Master arrives at the temple: a man to whom Morgan is immediately drawn both mentally and physically, a man who is strikingly familiar... yet utterly alien.

Year of the Ram is a fully-fleshed novel, approximately 97000 words, with a focus on the love story and romance angle. Set against a science fiction milieu, it explores the infinite possibilities of the human and alien heart. Sexual content is explicit, though is not the primary focus of the novel.

For those who like a romance that forces its characters to contemplate the ecstasies and the agonies of love... you will enjoy *Year of the Ram*.

www.eyescrypublications.com
Also on Amazon or order from your favorite bookseller.

All of our titles are available directly from our website, on Amazon, or may be ordered from most booksellers. Thanks for reading us!

Eye Scry Publications
A Visionary Publishing Company
www.eyescrypublications.com

www.ingramcontent.com/pod-product-compliance
Lightning Source LLC
Chambersburg PA
CBHW020318260626
47156CB00004B/1273